THE SEA BELOW

WILLIAM MEIKLE

SEVERED PRESS
HOBART TASMANIA

THE SEA BELOW

Copyright © 2021 By William Meikle

WWW.SEVEREDPRESS.COM

ISBN: 978-1-922551-83-2

- DANNY -

Danny arrived at the cave mouth far better prepared than he had been on his last trip here. Last time it had been a nightmare of plunging through watery darkness, evading a cave-wyrm in dark caverns and almost being buried under a mountain of stone, all done with limited supplies of booze and tobacco. This time he resolved to travel with at least a modicum of comforts.

The telegram from Stefan had been short, almost curt, but to the point.

"The lad has gone back down these two days now and there has since been no sign of him or his companions. Can you come?"

Danny had thought about it for all of a minute. Young Ed had come to him last time with a need for an adventurer-cum-bodyguard for a treasure hunt. They'd found, and lost said treasure, and Ed had also lost a brother. Danny wondered which of the two the lad was now searching for, and just how lost the young man might have got himself. It wasn't as if he was leaving behind any pressing engagements when he left London bound for Calais and points east that same afternoon; there are only so many old soldier's tales you can tell in the city taverns before the locals grow overly familiar with them. Likewise, he had few affairs to settle, having relied on his meagre army pension for the necessities of life. His only possessions were what he carried with him; his revolver, his saber, his sturdy boots and rugged clothes, and the contents of his pack. He'd spent most of what little savings he had on the contents, which consisted mainly of ammunition, tobacco, papers and matches, and liquor for his belly, something that had been sorely lacking last time round.

A large part of the liquor and tobacco was dispensed with on the journey on trains, boat and more trains, but he had replenished supplies in the inn before setting up the mountain trail and arrived at the cave mouth mostly penniless and as ready as he was ever going to be for what awaited him this time.

The journey had been a frustrating one of delays due to weather, broken-down trains and missed connections but all of that was forgotten in the welcome he received first from Elsa--a hot wet lick of the face from a German Shepherd dog made most things better--then from Stefan who gripped Danny's hand and shook it so violently he feared it might come off at the shoulder.

"Well met again, my friend," the shepherd said. "I only wish it were in better circumstances."

Acquaintance renewed, Stefan wasted no time in other pleasantries. He led Danny into the cave where it was immediately obvious that the way had been prepared in a far more engineered fashion than on their last visit. There were stout ropes and ladders in the passageways, oil lamps hanging, swinging in a slight breeze strung every three yards on a wire along the wall above head height, and wooden bridges across any parts that might otherwise have been perilous.

"The lad has been busy," Danny muttered.

"More than you know, my friend," Stefan replied.

The shepherd didn't elaborate, and didn't need to for Danny soon saw that young Edward's scheme of works in the cavern had been undertaken with a most definite purpose in mind. They arrived after a ten minute uphill walk that had taken the best part of an hour the last time, in the large cavern from where their descent into the lands below had begun. Two younger men sat at a camping stove. Stefan didn't really need to introduce them; it was obvious in their faces that they were all three related.

"My sister's boys," the shepherd explained. "They will wait here and raise an alarm should we, like Edward, fail to return."

There would be no need for a blind underwater descent on this occasion; the waterfall was no longer in evidence and more stout ropes led into the basin that had been a frothing pool, disappearing into the black dry pit that now showed there.

"He had the water diverted higher up," Stefan said when he saw Danny looking.

"Diverted to where?"

Stefan shrugged.

"I did not ask. All I know is that as soon as it ran dry the lad, two companions with him, was off and away down there, leaving me to wait. That was nigh on five days ago now."

"And there has been no communication since?"

"None. If you had not arrived today I would have gone down on my own, but now that you are here we can go together; it will be like old times."

"I bloody well hope not," Danny muttered, and eyed the dark pit with some degree of apprehension.

In the end the descent proved remarkably simple. Young Edward's engineering works had extended to an ingenious winch and pulley system that allowed for a controlled descent. A large wicker basket proved to be more than ample to allow Elsa to travel with them and it was not even necessary to descend in the dark, for the well-remembered glow of the bioluminescent vegetation was present after only a few yards down in the pit. The nightmare journey of the last time was forgotten. Danny had a smoke while Stefan's nephews did all the work with the winch in the cavern above and they went down at a calm, even pace towards the lands below.

After an uneventful trip of no more than ten minutes they descended out of the channel high above the underground lake. Danny had plenty of time to note that they were coming down into water again; that part couldn't be avoided. He flicked the butt of his smoke away and took out his revolver, raising it above his head as he went into the lake. The water only reached his hips and he was able to keep both his weapon, and his ammunition dry.

He noted that there was another winch and pulley system installed just above water level. They'd be able to use the basket to send up a message to the lads way above when, if, they were ready to return. The fact that Edward had not done so in the long days of his absence brought a fresh chill up Danny's spine as he unhooked himself from the harness. He looked up to see Elsa looking down at him. He swore that the dog was smiling. He didn't have to help her out of the basket; she waited until it was floating and then launched herself out, paddling for the shore at some speed.

Stefan was just seconds behind. The shepherd entered the water with less grace than the dog had managed but like Danny, he kept his rifle overhead and seconds later they were wading towards shore, each keeping an eye on the water, remembering the pale worm-like thing that had attacked them on their last visit.

No attack came. They reached shore safely and found their first indication that Edward and his companions had made it at least this far; there were signs that camp had been made on the rocky ground above the shore.

"Edward?" Stefan shouted, but Danny knew in his gut it wasn't going to be that simple. Elsa appeared to agree with him. She had run off some twenty yards down the slope and was now looking back at them, as if to admonish them for wasting time.

Danny motioned that Stefan should lead.

"Do you remember the way?"

"Every inch of it. It is seared in my memory. Is it not so with you?"

"In memory and in dreams," Danny replied. "Let us hope for happier instances of both this time around."

They headed off down the slope under the dim, all-pervading glow from the bioluminescent foliage on the roof above them.

They made good progress; the route was indeed impressed on their minds, and they had Elsa to follow if their memories should falter. They navigated the first series of caverns with no difficulty and nothing to impede them; there was no sign of any of the voracious predators they had encountered the last time. There was life however; a small flock of the pale, six-legged horse-like things scattered at their approach, and Elsa showed remarkable restraint every time they flushed the smaller, rabbit-like beasts from their hiding places.

They got their first indication they were on the right trail when they arrived at the cavern where Thomas Ellington had met his end. His fiery grave was now marked by a tall stone cairn topped with a rough wooden cross. Edward had been as good as his word and had returned to mark his brother's resting place properly.

They'd seen several of the great bats on their descent so far, and more of them hung here, bunched like a cluster of leathery fruit under the roof. They stirred listlessly overhead as Danny, Stefan and Elsa passed Tommy's cairn. Danny felt wetness drop onto his brow.

"The bloody things are pishing on us now."

He was tempted to shoot some of the beasts from their roost, just to teach them a lesson, but discretion proved stronger. Seconds later he felt another drip on his head and looked up to see only tangled, pale roots hanging above. On closer inspection he saw that the water appeared to be seeping out of the rock itself.

He thought no more of it and when they reached the end of that cavern and went down into a tunnel, the walls and floor were dry around them, although there was a faint, distant roar, like thunder heard far off on a summer's night.

They found more evidence of someone else having been in the caverns in a cave off the main channel; the remnants of a fire long since gone cold. It wasn't one of their making on their last trip, and was too long cold for it to have been Ed this time around; Danny could only surmise that it had been made by the ones that made the map Ed followed; the Templars who'd come down here to hide their treasure.

After a time they passed the skeletal remains of a great worm; they knew only too well the origins of this one. If he had a rummage among the bones Danny knew that he'd find several of his own bullets among them. They'd killed this bugger on their last trip, but at great cost.

"Do you think the lad has met another of these?" Stefan said, kicking at the bones.

"I bloody well hope not, for his sake," Danny replied.

Elsa pished on the pale skull as they passed. Danny quietly applauded the sentiment.

They were getting close to the deepest point they'd reached on their last trip, managing in a few hours what it had taken them more than a day the last time, when the thunder grew louder above them, a roar that seemed to fill the cavern.

"What's this shite now?" Danny said. Elsa growled, as if in agreement.

Water dripped from the roof and Danny realised the rock underfoot was wet now, and getting wetter. They were in a steeply sloping cavern, heading down to where Danny knew it opened out to an inland sea some distance below. He wished he could remember how far it might be for the water underfoot was coming faster, a stream that was threatening to become a river.

"Quickly," he said, "we need to get out of this sharpish before it gets worse."

They broke into a trot, splashing through running water that felt cold around their ankles. The thunder rose, and rose again until they couldn't hear their splashing above its roar. The current got stronger, threatening to topple them, and more water ran from the roof such that it was like running through a rainstorm.

Danny looked up to see a rough oval of light far below them.

"Faster!" he shouted, and put on a burst of speed he didn't know he had in him. The water built up around them until they were being pushed more than they were running. They emerged out of the cave seconds later like a cork out of a shaken bottle. Danny threw himself to one side of the cave mouth as the roar became a crescendo and a wall of water blew in a spout out and over the cliff face. He tumbled, flailing arms and legs, then slid on his arse down a wet scree slope before coming to a halt, bruised, battered and alive, barely, on the rocky shore of the inland sea.

Elsa licked at his face, Stefan groaned somewhere to his left, and the shadow of something apart from his companions fell over him. He was reaching for his pistol when a well-remembered voice spoke from above him.

"Captain Daniel Garland as I live and breathe? What in blazes are you doing here?"

Danny reached up a hand and let young Edward Ellington help him to his feet.

They'd found their quarry at the first time of asking.

- ED -

Ed was surprised to see the soldier, less so to find Stefan and the dog alongside him. He'd been meaning to return up through the caverns and get a message up top for several days now but there had just been so much to do, so many preparations to make and time had got away from him. He tried to explain it to the new arrivals as they sat around a fire while a pot of coffee brewed.

"It was when I realised that the treasure was lost to us that I made up my mind," he said while Danny rolled a smoke. He motioned over, past where water still gushed out of the cave mouth, to a wall of what looked like recently tumbled rock. "You remember the serpent and the hoard? Of course you do. Well it's under there now, several hundred feet under there. That cause is hopeless. We couldn't get at it if we tried, not even with a hundred men; we'd bring the roof down around us at the first attempt."

"So why are you still here?" Danny asked. "What did you make up your mind to do?"

Ed pointed the other way along the shore. His two companions were a hundred yards away in that direction, the sounds of axes on wood carrying clearly across the still air between them.

"We're building canoes. I mean to explore this sea."

He had to give both Danny and Stefan time to calm down after that revelation, as both the older men obviously saw no merit in the idea.

"I didn't come all this way to go fishing with you, lad," Danny said. "The Lord only knows what dangers might await out there."

"And that's exactly why I plan to go," Ed replied. "There are islands out there, I saw them from high up on the cliff when I was exploring. A whole archipelago waiting to be found. Think on it."

"I am thinking about it," Danny said. "That's the problem. I'd prefer a few tankards of ale back in the inn though."

Ed laughed.

"I'll admit that sounds enticing, and I would gladly join you. I owe it to Tommy...I owe it to myself. I will go on. However, I cannot ask you to accompany me. You are welcome to go back. But I believe it has become a moot point in any case; our return passage is closed to us." He motioned back to the cave mouth from which water spouted in an arc over the cliff. "Sheer pressure of water alone would be enough to prevent any egress by that route."

"That will soon run dry," Danny said and Ed laughed again.

"I believe not. You see, when I had the water diverted above the waterfall, I had a feeling that I was merely postponing the inevitable; water finds its way to the lowest point, in time. It seems that this is the lowest point, and that time has arrived."

"You mean we're stuck here? Again?" Danny said.

"No, my friend, we are not stuck. We are, as you said, going fishing."

After coffee and a smoke, Ed took the new arrivals along the shore to the spot that had been home for him and the others for the last week. He introduced them to his companions, Bill and George, two soft-spoken, quiet English youths who Ed had spent the summer climbing with in the Alps. The youths eyed Danny's pistol and saber warily but quickly warmed to the man once Ed explained his friendship.

Introductions done, Ed showed Danny the progress so far.

Three rough huts had been built high on the shore. In front of them lay two long, wide canoes hewn out of the wood of the thick-rooted vegetation that passed as trees down here.

"We had to look a long way down the coast to find large enough specimens for the job, and they were a bugger to hollow out. But they float just fine, they're totally waterproof. They'll get the job done," Ed said, seeing that Danny was still skeptical of the whole affair. "We have paddles, we have rough fishing rods, even some bait. We've caught enough of the rabbit-things to have a plentiful supply of dried meat for the trip, we still have rations in our packs, and if there are any big predators in the water, we have yet to see them. We can do this."

"And nothing has attacked you in the days you've been here?"

"Just the bats," Ed answered. "And they've kept away since we shot three of them down that first time they showed up."

The one thing that seemed to please Danny was that Ed had come prepared on this trip. He'd insisted that all three of them be armed with both pistols and hunting rifles and Ed himself had a large knife--more akin to a small sword--strapped to his belt. The only thing he'd used it for so far had been to hack at vegetation, but he felt better for having it close by him at all times.

He'd lost Danny's attention again; the old soldier's gaze kept turning to the spout of water and the cave mouth, as if willing the flow to lessen but Ed could see that the opposite was happening. The waterfall had done nothing but gain strength since ejecting Danny and Stefan, and the whole side of the cliff below its exit point had started to flake and crumble away under the pressure.

"There is really no other way back?" Stefan said.

Ed shook his head.

"The way up to the surface that we took from the treasure room is buried under a mountain of rock. And I have walked the shore miles in each direction from here to no avail. It's the sea or nothing."

"Nothing it is then," Danny said under his breath.

"So what makes you think there's going to be anything more than more of the same to find out there?" Danny said later when they were once again sitting around a fire drinking coffee.

"What makes you think there isn't?" Ed replied. "Aren't we here to explore?"

"You might be. I'm here to save your arse," Danny replied.

"In case you haven't noticed, I'm a big boy now, Danny," Ed replied. "I'm sorry I was remiss in sending news back of our endeavors here, and I'm sorry that decision has got you stuck down here with me. But as you can see, I don't need saving."

"That's a matter of opinion."

"Look, wait here if you want. But by my watch it's time for a kip, and when we wake, Bill, George and I will be taking to the water. Come or stay, it matters not to me."

Ed saw the displeasure on Danny's face but took little heed of it. He'd come on this trip for two reasons; firstly to give his brother Tommy a proper burial, and secondly to attempt to recover the lost treasure. He'd succeeded at one, failed at the other. But adventure and exploration were more than enough compensation, for him anyway. A jaded old soldier was not going to hold him back.

He still felt the same in what passed for a morning. Danny and Stefan were still sitting by the fire and smoking; they might have been there since Ed took to his hut for all he knew. Danny was still in somewhat of a huff and it was Stefan who spoke.

"We have talked it over," the shepherd said. "And we have had a look at our options. It seems you are right; there is no way back. We will accompany you on the water, if you will have us?"

"Of course we will have you, and we'll be happy of the company. It will be more cramped than I would like, but I will take a canoe with Bill, George and half the provisions if you take the other?"

Stefan nodded.

"Boats and I are strangers to each other, but Danny says he knows their ways. We will be fine."

They loaded the canoes and launched with little fanfare half an hour later.

It proved to be relatively easy going. The surface of the underground sea kept perfectly still with not even the hint of a breeze; Ed was able to look down into crystal clear depths and see pale, wafting vegetation many yards below them, a washed-out gray version of the kelps he'd seen off the Orkney coast while climbing on Hoy.

Bill and George took first dibs on the paddling, leaving Ed free to keep lookout in the prow. His main job was to call out if it looked like they might stray from the line-of-sight course he'd decided on. It was not a difficult line to follow. The island that was their destination could not be seen from their position on the water, but there was a darker patch of roof that provided an ever-present landmark for him to fix on.

Behind them, Stefan and Danny were also paddling smoothly, both with cigarettes stuck in the side of their mouth while Elsa mimicked Ed's lookout position sitting up proud in the prow of the second canoe. The dog was the only one of the three who looked happy.

The shore they'd left was already receding away behind them and it was not too long before it could not be distinguished from the cliff wall at its back. Several of the great bats spiralled high up some distance away and Ed eyed them warily but the beasts showed no indication that they were interested in the canoes and they too were soon lost in the distance behind them.

It was a strangely silent journey. There were no bird calls, no splash of feeding fish and indeed no insect life of any kind that Ed could notice. Several times he bent over the prow to look down into the depths but there was no life to note there either. There was only the slowly wafting fronds of pale vegetation. The only thing of note was the fact that the air became noticeably warmer the further they got from shore and Bill and George had soon worked up a sweat despite the easy going. When he noted that, Ed called for a break. The two canoes came together side by side and Ed shared water from one of their canteens.

"So far, so tedious. How distant are these bally islands?" Danny asked.

"By my ready reckoning, we're about a third of the way there," Ed replied. "But distances are deceptive down here in this strange light. I might be half an hour out either way but another two hours feels about right."

"Let us hope it is less. These canoes float well enough but my arse has gone to sleep and my old knees might never be the same again."

Stefan laughed at that, and fetched a small deerskin from his bag on the bottom of the vessel.

"Then have some of this, old friend," he said. "It cures all the ills of men as old as we have become."

It wasn't water that the shepherd shared but a fiery brandy-like liquor that Ed only sipped at, for it was heady stuff. Danny took to it with some gusto though, and had a healthier color in his cheeks when Ed announced it was time to get going.

Ed took over paddling duty from Bill for the next phase of the journey and soon fell into an almost trance-like rhythm where all that existed was the metronomic sweep and tug of the paddle against the water. He was surprised when Bill tapped him on the shoulder and pointed forward.

The islands were in view in the distance. The darker patch that was his sightline was above the right-hand end and the whole archipelago in that direction lay in deeper shadows. Ed decided to aim instead for a lighter spot farther to the left, where the land appeared to be dense in vegetation.

He called for another water break and they brought the canoes together again.

Ed pointed out the new destination.

"Let us hope there is a tavern," Danny said. "Although my old bones might be too tired to accommodate any dancing girls, at least not tonight."

Bill took over from George for the last stage and on this stretch, Ed couldn't quite lose himself in the rhythm for as the island drew ever closer, he felt the excitement of the explorer rise up in him.

He paddled faster, eager for land.

- DANNY -

They were still four hundred yards from what looked to be a rocky shore when Elsa barked loudly. She wasn't looking forward but off to the port side and when Danny looked in that direction it was just in time to see a pale tail fluke slip under the surface some forty yards distant. The tail itself was as wide as one of the canoes was long. It slid beneath the surface with barely a splash.

Danny had been in whale waters before and knew only too well the dangers that could be posed for small craft such as theirs--and that was even before considering whether the beast he'd just seen was carnivorous or not, or even a whale at all.

He looked forward to the canoe ahead to see that Ed had also taken note of the beast.

"To shore," Danny shouted. "Double time."

He put his shoulders into paddling and between them he and Stefan put on a burst of speed that had them catching the canoe ahead. The beast resurfaced again on the starboard side several minutes later, closer now, as if curious. Danny caught a good long look at a high back that was ridged and rough, more crocodile-like than whale.

The back rose, the tail came up then it was gone again. Given the way the fluke had risen up, Danny knew the beast had made only a shallow dive.

"Eyes open, Shepherd," he said. "There's a beastie on the prowl."

It could be anywhere, perhaps even underneath them. That thought gave even more impetus to his paddling and the water churned around them as they sped across the surface. Danny saw that the canoe ahead was likewise sending up slapping splashes of water. Too late, he realised that their activity, far from speeding them to safety, might actually be what was drawing the beast towards them.

"Stop," he shouted. "Quiet."

But his revelation had come too late. The canoe ahead rose up prow first out of the water, driven upward by something from below. The vessel tipped over, dumping the three men overboard and into the sea where they splashed and yelled, drawing even more attention to themselves.

"Quiet, you fools," Danny shouted, aware that he was breaking his own advice. He indicated to Stefan that they should go to the three men's aid and turned the canoe toward them. They were still five yards distant when the beast came up again, massive maw first, a dark mouth filled with ivory-pale, pencil thin teeth that clamped around Bill's waist. Blood darkened the water, Bill yelled, just once, more in confusion than pain, then he was gone leaving only a bloody froth of bubbles at the surface. Looking down, Danny saw a gray serpent-like shape descend away from them at speed.

Danny leaned forward to help Ed up out of the water.

"Our packs," the younger man shouted. "Get our packs first."

Stefan had already hauled one of the packs, sodden and heavy with water, up into the bottom of the canoe. Danny reached for the other and saw that George, rather than try to get back into the other canoe, was swimming with strong strokes towards the shore that was now less than a hundred yards distant.

"Come back, you bloody fool," Danny shouted but got no reply. The other man continued to swim strongly shoreward.

"Bloody young fool. He's going to get himself eaten."

It only took them seconds to discover that the first canoe had been badly damaged in the attack and was already lying deeper in the water, starting to sink.

"All aboard who's coming aboard," Danny muttered, and helped Stefan drag a sodden Ed up out of the water and into their canoe which was itself now overburdened and sluggish to their paddling.

"Softly now," Danny said. "We make for shore, but quietly, Slow, steady strokes, no splashing."

Ed was looking over the side into the depths.

"Bill?" he whispered.

"He's gone, lad," Danny said. "And we're likely to be too in short order if we don't get out of the water."

They paddled, quietly as Danny had asked, although the temptation to put on a spurt of speed grew ever more insistent in Danny's mind as they approached the shore. All three were casting glances more to the water than to the shore, expecting at any minute for the beast to resurface and take renewed interest in them. Danny eventually looked shoreward to see George pull himself out of the water and up onto the stones where he dropped as if in exhaustion to the ground.

The next time Danny looked shoreward they were only ten yards from where George stood at the water's edge facing them. Behind the younger man, some ten yards farther up the shore, a forest of pale leafy vegetation loomed, a wall as high as twenty feet in places.

"Come on," George shouted, waving them forward.

In response to his call the branches seemed to come alive as if hit by a strong wind, branches thrashing and loose leaves scattering in the air. A raucous howling rose up, a cacophony of barking and yelping.

"What the blazes is this now?" Danny muttered.

Beasts came out of the trees, a troop of what at first glance looked to be pale baboons, each as big as a large dog, barrel chested and massive jawed, lips pulled back and grinning as they showed too many teeth. As if propelled by a soundless command they all had their gazes fixed on the young man on the shore. As they left the forest they broke into a run. Danny just had time to note that they, like all creatures they'd seen here in the deep places, bore six limbs then he'd dropped the paddle and was struggling to unholster his pistol.

He was far too late and knew it before metal left leather. Young George never knew what hit him; he was still facing the water when the first of the apes reached him. It leapt, back legs propelling it high onto the lad's back, its weight toppling him forward. Once he was down there was no chance of him getting back up. The beasts swarmed over him, teeth and clawed fingers biting and digging. Black rod went red as blood flew in the air, sending the beasts into even more frenzy. They tore at the body in fury. George's screams were mercifully brief.

It was mere seconds after the attack that Stefan and Danny fired in unison. The result was immediate. Two of the beasts fell and the rest scattered back into the trees and were gone as swiftly as they had come. But it was too little, too late for George. His dead eyes watched them accusingly as they beached the canoe and stepped warily ashore.

- ED -

Stefan and Danny went straight to check on the prone man, but Ed didn't move from beside the canoe; he knew already that their checks would be fruitless; George's eyes told all the story he needed to hear.

"Still think exploration is worth the risk, lad?" Danny said bitterly as he stood from George's body.

Ed didn't, couldn't, reply. He looked, from the body, to the sea where Bill had vanished, then back to the body, unable to come to terms with the fact that both his friends had gone within minutes of each other, suddenly and without a goodbye, leaving Ed soaked and cold, alone on this rocky shore far from anywhere he might find solace.

"We need to bury him," Ed said. Danny and Stefan were busy dragging the canoe up what passed for a beach, while Elsa stood guard, her gaze on the trees, a deep growl rumbling in her throat. "We need to say some words."

"What we need to do is find a safe spot, and sharpish," Danny said. "We don't know how many of yon ape-things there are about here. If they come back in force, they'll run over us, guns or no guns."

"We can't just leave him lying on the shore," Ed said. "I won't leave him."

Danny hefted one of the packs from the bottom of the canoe.

"That's your choice, of course. But I'm taking off. It's him or these," the soldier said. "I'm sorry, lad, but these will do us more good. Loath as I am to leave a fallen man behind, we are in no position to carry him away; there is too much peril in that course. I first came along with you last year to protect you. This is me doing my job. Now come on, at the double. We've done enough jawing here already."

But even as Danny was turning away, the violent shaking of the foliage started again, accompanied by a cacophony of high barks and wails. Given the extent of the thrashing Ed thought that this whole stretch of shoreline must be infested with the baboons. Elsa barked as two larger individuals dropped out of the foliage to stand upright, not moving, but keeping their gaze on the men on the shore.

Ed had his first good look at the things that had killed his friend. Baboon was indeed the closest approximation he could come up with although these seemed stockier, more barrel chested than he would have thought. All six limbs were knotted with muscle and the heavy jaws looked more akin to that of a wolf than any monkey, teeth looking disproportionally large in relation to the mouth. Pale blue eyes stared directly at Ed, sending a cold shiver up his spine.

They looked hungry.

- DANNY -

"I don't fancy having a running fight along the beach," Danny said. "I suggest we retreat back into the canoe… we can stick close to shore and look for a safe harbor."

"Then let us hope these beasts have not learned how to swim," Stefan said. The shepherd was having to hold Elsa back; the dog was prepared to launch herself at the two watching beasts given a chance.

"What about George?" Ed said.

"There's no room in the canoe," Danny said baldly. He saw that the younger man was hurting, but Ed needed to hear the truth. It was going to be a hard lesson for him to learn. "And perhaps leaving him will serve a purpose; it may keep the baboons off us long enough for us to get away."

He saw the implication hit Ed hard.

"You mean to leave him as food?"

The last word was shouted, a wail of pain. The baboons reacted with screams of their own and when Danny looked over it was to see six of them now standing at the edge of the foliage. It would only take one of them to break ranks for a charge to begin.

"There's no time to argue, lad," he said and turned to Stefan. "Get the gear back in the canoe. We're leaving."

The shepherd was wise enough to the situation to not argue and hurried to comply. Ed, however, stepped over and stood before the body of his friend.

"Can we at least put him in the water, out at sea? I cannot stand the thought of these beasts having him."

"And would you rather feed yon sea serpent instead?" Danny said, attempting to use the bluntness to get Ed to move, but immediately sorry for the new pain he saw cross the lad's face. He spoke softly. "Come away, lad, or we'll all be joining your pal here soon enough."

Danny helped Stefan get the packs in the canoe, Elsa leapt in to claim the prow position and they pushed the laden vessel back down the beach to the water's edge, its bottom rasping and grating against the rocky foreshore.

When Danny looked back, Ed was still standing over George's body, tears streaming down his cheeks. He didn't even have his weapon in hand. Past the lad, Danny saw that more than a dozen baboons had massed in two ranks at the foliage's edge. They shrieked and chattered and he knew it was only a matter of time before they egged each other into an attack; a gang was a gang, no matter what the species.

Danny took out his pistol, took aim, and dropped the largest one, hoping to repeat the scattering flight of the last time. This time the beasts held their ground, roaring as one and thrashing at the ground with their paws.

"Ed, it's now or never," Danny shouted and with a push launched the canoe completely into the water. The baboons roared and broke into a charge.

Ed fled in the face of their teeth and talons and almost threw himself into the canoe. Stefan paddled but Danny took several seconds before joining him, downing three more of the charging beasts before holstering his pistol and taking up a paddle. When he looked back it was to see the baboons gathered in a frenzied mass over their dead, blood flying in a fine spray in the air as they tore at flesh and limbs. Young George was in there somewhere too, but thankfully the press of bodies of the baboons obscured his final fate.

When he turned back away from the gory feast it was to see that the canoe was pointing back out to the deeper water.

"Turn in," Danny called out. "We'll stay ten yards from shore, no more, no less. Too shallow for the serpent, too deep for the baboons."

"And I'll say it again. What if they can swim?" Stefan asked as the canoe turned to travel parallel to the shore.

Danny laughed.

"That's the least of our worries. If they get in the water, they'll be slow, we can pick them off one at a time. And who knows, maybe yon serpent will do the job for us; I'll take all the help we can get."

They paddled parallel to the shore for almost an hour, again using the darker patch on the roof above as their line of sight. Ed sat at the rear and didn't speak, didn't even take a smoke when Danny offered. Danny eyed the shore warily all the way. For a while he thought the island might be uniformly covered with the dense vegetation, which in turn appeared to be also uniformly inhabited by more of the baboons, but after a time the foliage was broken up by rocky outcrops and cliffs, and soon after that the land rose higher, became stonier. It looked even less hospitable than the forest, despite the lack of baboons.

"We might have to go back the way we came and take our chances with yon serpent-thing,"

Danny said after a time when they'd seen little but bare rock. "There's nowt for us here."

Elsa barked as if in agreement, but when Danny looked forward, he saw she had her gaze focussed on a promontory several hundred yards ahead. It was almost an island, joined to the shore by a low rocky beach, but the thing that had Danny struck almost dumb was the fact that it was not just bare rock; it was, or had been, a fortified dwelling, a high circle of thick stone walls rising high above the water, open to the sky on the roofline, like a truncated cone.

The sight of the stone structure ahead appeared to bring Ed out of the blue funk that had taken him since they'd lost Bill and George, the tingle and thrill of exploration almost, but not quite, intruding on his grief.

"I've seen structures like this before, they call them brochs in the Orkney Isles north of Scotland, ancient fortifications against sea raiders," Ed said, his first words since they'd got into the canoe. "I never expected to find the like here, so far from the worlds of men."

"You and me both, lad," Danny replied. "But it's the first place we've seen that might be defensible; my arse thinks it's dead again in this bloody canoe, so I'm all for heading ashore and giving it a once over. Are you with me?"

Ed nodded, and Danny took that as a yes. They paddled for shore.

Elsa was out of the water and paddling for the rocky outcrop before they got within ten yards of it, and by the time they beached the canoe below what appeared to be a doorway, the dog was already inside exploring. Danny left Stefan and Ed to lug the packs out of the canoe and went to find the dog.

She was sitting inside the circular walls with a dead rabbit in her mouth, looking very pleased with herself.

"Shelter and supper, what more does a man need," Danny muttered.

It didn't take Danny long to see that there was no other life on the rock. Inside the broch they were safe from attack most of the way around, shielded by a twelve-foot high wall. It was broken only on the side nearest the main island by a thin doorway that could be closed with a door of the same wood as the canoe they'd arrived in, and held closed by a sliding lock of more of the same wood. The wood had been smoothed by ages of use but the circular fire pit in the center of the building was long cold and the place had the air of having been abandoned for a great many years, perhaps even centuries.

"So, do we stay?" Stefan asked as he and Ed arrived with the packs.

"Aye. It can be secured. We'll have to keep watch of course, but it's far better than either the beach or the canoe. We can defend this."

Danny left Stefan and Ed to get a fire going with what they could find around the broch while he went in search of a longer term supply of combustible material. Elsa came along at his side as they made their way across the rough stones that connected the promontory to the main island. There was more evidence of the rabbit-like things here; droppings were droppings wherever you found them, but no sign of anything larger than that.

The walkway led to a rising track up onto a hill, which gave Danny a view over this end of the island. Away to his left he saw that a rocky plateau bounded onto the forest of the pale vegetation that harbored the baboons. The plateau itself was mostly rock and sparse grasses with the occasional larger shrub dotted across it; he'd seen the same pattern in many of the caverns they'd descended through higher above, and was not too surprised to see a small herd of a score of the six-legged horses galloping away from his position at some speed.

To his right the island stretched away into a dim distance, darker there under a rock ceiling that was not festooned with the bioluminescent vegetation that had been ubiquitous everywhere else. Dark towers appeared to rise up on the horizon, although whether they were structures like the broch or the remnants of long dead trees he could not tell at this distance.

Besides, he wasn't here to gawk. He was pleased to see that, also as in the higher caverns, there was plenty of the dead and dry tinder just lying around for the taking. They would have fire as long as they wanted it. With that, and the water from the inland sea which was drinkable, if somewhat metallic to the taste, they could survive on the rations they were carrying for some time to come. And if Elsa could continue to bring home the rabbits, so much the better.

Danny was feeling slightly better about their situation as he carried the first of several armfuls of tinder back to their new home.

- ED -

Curiosity about the structure around him finally intruded on Ed's grief after Stefan lit a fire and boiled up water for coffee. The shepherd stood at the doorway watching out for Danny's return, leaving Ed free to examine their new surroundings.

The masonry was of the highest quality; he'd be pushed to insert a cigarette paper in any of the cracks, despite there being no evidence of mortar. The more he looked the more he was struck by the similarity to the brochs of Orkney, although here the rock was more porous, more volcanic in nature than the rough slate deployed by the Orcadians. And if his estimate was right, this structure was older by far than those on the wind-swept coastline far above and to the west. There was a sense of great age in these stones that had Ed wondering if the people who erected them had even been modern men at all. Neanderthals had lived in caves not fifty miles from this one; was it beyond the bounds of possibility that they had infiltrated here too, and left works by which they could be remembered?

Whoever they were, they had employed fire, that was obvious in the extra blackening of the walls and the stones in the central firepit. They had also been remarkably neat and tidy, for there were no artefacts, not even animal or fish bones. Ed wondered if the place had been a dwelling at all, or rather had it been a building of some kind of spiritual import, like a temple? His suspicions in that direction grew stronger when he examined the section of wall opposite the doorway. On close inspection he saw that it was covered with rank after rank of tiny carved figurines, each no more than the length of Ed's thumb, stick men--or rather, stick figures, for these, although they appeared to be bi-pedal and upright, all had six limbs. The figures depicted all had some kind of disability or injury--no head, one limb missing, one leg missing, both legs missing, row after row of them covering a six-foot breadth and the full height of the wall in serried ranks.

It obviously had meant something to whoever had carved them there, but Ed couldn't make head nor tail of it.

He fetched a notebook and pencil from his pack and began to copy down as many of the ranks as he could make out. He was still at it when Danny returned with the first armful of kindling and a report as to what he'd seen from the hill above the shore.

"No more monkeys?" Stefan asked, and Danny laughed.

"No, friend. I fear there's no food to their liking up this end of the island, which may prove to be both a good and a bad thing for us, for we too must eat."

They decided on coffee before Danny ventured out again and all three sat, drank and smoked in silence for a time, watching Stefan turn the rabbit on a makeshift spit before the shepherd took out his deerskin of liquor.

He handed it to Ed.

"We cannot bury them, but we should say a word for your friends, don't you think?"

Ed took a deep slug before replying.

"Yes, they were my friends," he said. "And I am right sore to have brought them to this end. I only hope they will be able to rest easy where they lie, for it is a great shame to have left them as we did."

"Had we not, we would be lying alongside them," Danny said softly. "It is always the way for those who survive."

Danny took the deerskin from Ed and raised it as if in toast.

"To absent friends," he said, and took a draught that would have floored Ed.

Stefan took the deerskin, took a drink as long again, then surprised Ed by bursting into song, a sad lament in German in a clear, high baritone that rang and echoed around the broch as if it was a natural amphitheatre, the shepherd's echoing voice taking on a resonance and depth that was almost religious. Ed felt fresh tears come and turned away towards the figures on the wall again lest the others see, losing himself for a time in the routine of copying the ranks into his notebook.

He was surprised to look up some time later to see Danny arriving in the doorway again with another armful of tinder; he had not noticed the old soldier leaving.

"That should see us through until morning," Danny said. "Or at least until what passes for morning in these parts. I don't know about you chaps but it feels to me like it's time to be abed. It seems like a mighty long age since I last slept."

Ed nodded.

"I have noticed since I arrived in this place that I have to remind myself to take a rest," he said. "In a place with no day or night one must make their own sense of time."

"For my part I am used to the cycles of sun and moon. I feel them in my blood, and my blood says it is the middle of the night somewhere overhead. I shall take first watch," Stefan said. "A shepherd is used to being vigilant while others sleep. But first, eating is also required."

They shared the rabbit among them, Elsa getting an equal portion to the men. They washed it down with some of Stefan's liquor, and after a smoke, Ed felt a wave of exhaustion wash over him. Using his pack as a pillow he lay down at the fireside and attempted to calm his mind enough to allow sleep. At first his thoughts were a roil of confusion; visions of death and bloody violence, red in tooth and claw and his grief surged back in full to almost overwhelm him. Desperate to seek solace anywhere else, his thoughts turned to the ranks of figures he had been transcribing. They marched across the mirror of his mind like a tiny army and, similar to the old trick of counting sheep, he found a strange comfort and restfulness in them, so much so that they were still with him there in the dark, marching in time as he finally fell into the well of sleep and welcome darkness.

He was woken sometime later by Danny shaking him by the shoulder.

"Your turn, lad. Best take my pistol. I've laid yours out to dry near the fire; you forgot that you took a soaking before we got you onto yon beach."

Ed rose groggily, the pistol feeling like a dead weight at the end of his arm as he half-walked, half-staggered to the doorway, not fully waking until he got some fresher air in his face from outside.

Danny lay down by the fire and was snoring several minutes later. Stefan likewise was off in the land of Nod but Elsa was wide awake and on guard at Ed's feet, intently looking out over the causeway to the main island.

Nothing moved and scarcely a breath of wind stirred the air. Ed's gaze rose when something higher up caught his eye. A flock of the great bats flew overhead, scores of them, all moving with an apparently singular purpose, heading directly for the darker area far to the right where the light dimmed and shadows gathered. Not for the first time Ed wondered at the extent of the ecosystem that appeared to be thriving down here so far from the eyes of the scientific community. He'd come here at first as a boy in search of treasure but now he thought, as a man, of the advances in knowledge he might impart to the world could he only escape to bring the news out.

Here, on an island in a seemingly endless sea, stranded under God alone knew how many tons of rock, escape seemed a distant prospect.

His watch proved to be uneventful. Elsa appeared to agree, and had laid down to sleep at his feet. Ed's attention turned once more to the stick figures. The implications were almost too much for his mind to hold. If it was more than some artistic license, if the people who drew these things were representing themselves, then there was, or had been, a race of six-limbed humanoids here in the depths of the earth, a parallel form of evolution that would surely have stumped Darwin as much as it stumped Ed. And once again his thoughts turned to what purpose the figures had served. Were they ceremonial in nature? Or were they some kind of record, marking time like a calendar? It was a code his mind continued to strain at, but when Stefan rose and began to prepare coffee some hours later, Ed was no closer to cracking it.

He put it from his mind completely when Danny woke and their talk turned to less esoteric notions, the matter of their survival.

They were breaking their fast with bread and cheese from Stefan's seemingly bottomless shepherd's bag. Danny spoke up first.

"We'll do okay for a few days, weeks even," he said. "But once the rations we brought in are gone the fare may become somewhat monotonous. Elsa may be needed to hunt rabbits for us, and we can try fishing, but I don't hold much hope in that regard, for the waters looked to be mightily empty save for yon big serpent thing. We are lucky in that we have a defensible shelter, but I fear it is in the wrong place for it to be a long-term solution."

Ed looked up as he lit a smoke.

"You want to move on?"

"Not yet," Danny said. "But we should explore outwards from here as much as we can, maybe go out a few hours in each direction, and return here for sleep."

"We should all go together," Stefan said. "A shepherd does not split his flock in unknown territory."

"Agreed," Danny said. "That was my plan in any case. We will trust to fate and leave the bulk of our packs here behind a closed door. That way we can travel light and be unencumbered should haste be needed."

Danny didn't say why haste might be needed. He didn't have to, for Ed's imagination was more than capable of filling in the blanks.

-DANNY-

Danny took the lead when they left the broch twenty minutes later. He decided on a direct line across the island for this first outing; he already knew there were baboons to his left and he wasn't keen to enter the darker gloom far to the right, at least not until he had a better idea of the lie of the land.

Without the burden of a pack, with his saber swinging at his side and his pistol at his hip, he felt more like the soldier he had been and he even had a tingle of anticipation at the prospect of what might lie ahead. He felt alive, and that was something he'd been missing since joining civilian ranks these two years past. He could have asked for better circumstances than being stranded in these caverns, but all things considered, it was a great deal preferable to being dead.

"Better even than surviving in London," he muttered. "But I could murder a flagon of ale right now."

Elsa foraged ahead of them, as keen as ever to flush out any of the rabbit-things that proved more curious than cautious, but Danny stopped the others as they crested the small hill he'd climbed before to allow them a view over the rocky landscape they would be traversing.

"Good Lord," Ed said. "It is certainly bigger than I thought. But will it all be like this? Dry and mostly dead?"

Danny laughed.

"It's no Isle of Wight, that's for sure. But yon baboons have thrived well enough here, have they not? Where monkeys can live, so can we."

Stefan was looking right at the gloom under the darker patch of roof.

"Are those dwellings over there?"

All three turned to look, but no amount of attempted peering would enable them to discern the exact nature of the taller things in the shadows.

"We'll get to them eventually," Danny said. "First things first. I'd like to find a supply of better water. And maybe some bigger game that would be preferable to stringy rabbit. Come. The day, such as it is, is passing."

The first hour of their expedition passed uneventfully. The terrain proved to be as bleak as Danny had feared, a wide expanse of the same basaltic rock and scattered shrubs. Elsa got excited at one point when she finally flushed a rabbit from hiding, but it was too fast for her and it disappeared into a crack in the rock too narrow for her to follow.

They stopped for a drink and a smoke on another small hill. From this vantage they saw that the island rose higher ahead to a tall conical mountain that might have been a volcano in some distant past. Some two miles away in that direction, where the slope got steepest, the bare rock gave way to a forest of pale vegetation that stretched away and up to a treeline just below the top. Danny was still looking upwards when Ed grabbed at his arm and pointed to the right-hand side of the slopes. This time there was no doubt about it; a score of dwellings, broch-like structures that seemed to mimic the cone of the dead volcano above, dotted the lower slope at the spot where the forest took over from rock.

"We need to investigate," Ed said.

"I guess we do," Danny replied, but he was eyeing the forest rather than the brochs, hoping for some of that larger game he'd mentioned earlier.

They got their first sign there might be better hunting ahead when Elsa discovered a pile of droppings that needed to be pissed on. Stefan bent and prodded at the faeces with a stick. The stench that wafted up from them had both Danny and Ed stepping back with hands covering their mouths.

"Please don't do that again," Ed said as Stefan rose, laughing.

"Some kind of deer I think," the shepherd said. "Bigger than rabbit, smaller than those horse-things we've seen."

"Not baboon?" Danny asked.

Stefan shook his head.

"They are meat eaters. There's no meat in these droppings, just plant matter."

"I'll take your word for it," Danny said, and stood back even more.

They found more of the same kind of droppings over the next half hour as they neared where the land rose. Elsa did her business on each of them and Stefan thankfully refrained from poking around but the smell still hung heavy in the still, warm air. Danny chain smoked, the tobacco doing a fine job of keeping the stench at bay. There were no flies around, in keeping with the seeming lack of insect life in these depths, a small mercy for which to be thankful as the air got warmer still the closer they approached to the forested area.

The volcano wasn't the tallest that Danny had seen on his travels but the slopes were steep and as they approached the tree line all three of them were working up a sweat with the effort of climbing.

They had been tacking rightwards ever since seeing the brochs and approached the dwellings cautiously. There was no sign that they had been inhabited in recent memory. The forest had engulfed many of them, tumbled ruins that could be seen among the foliage; there was no smoke of campfires, no livestock, just a deep stillness, not even a breeze disturbing the air. And if there were deer in the area, they too were keeping their heads down.

"It feels like the whole land is holding its breath," Ed said in a whisper, as if afraid to pierce the calm with noise. The silence felt somehow even more profound when they reached the brochs and wandered among them. These too had been uninhabited for a great age, only dry stone and cold hearths left behind. Unlike their new home on the shore, there was at least evidence of long-term habitation here; piles of animal bone that may have been deer and rabbit lay on the ground, and one massive skull mounted on a wall had Danny's old army senses tingling; it had been a great predator in its day given the breadth of its jaw and the size of its teeth, although he could not match it with anything in his experience.

Young Ed seemed to be more interested in the walls than the bones.

"There are no carvings here," he said, appearing to be disappointed.

"Aye, and no food either," Danny replied. "But a settlement like this must have got water from somewhere. I suggest we find it. Then I'd like to start back; we've come far enough for a first day's exploration."

Elsa proved her worth once again by being the member of the small expedition most capable of sniffing out water. On Stefan's urging she led them to the edge of the settlement farthest from the forested area and started pawing at the ground. Ten seconds of moving away tumbled pebbles uncovered an ancient well dug deep into the ground, the walls formed with the same stone as the brochs, fortified by what looked to be a rough muddy clay. Danny dropped a pebble down the hole. The splash came back almost immediately; there was water no more than six feet below them. With Stefan holding his legs, Danny went over the edge and down carrying an empty canteen. He was easily able to reach downward and fill the container before allowing himself to be dragged ungainly back up to the others.

He sniffed at the water first, then let Elsa do the same to some of it in the palm of his hand. She sniffed twice, then lapped it up with her tongue, her tail wagging at the same time.

"I'll take that as a yes then," Danny said.

He looked down at the well.

"Mark the spot," he said. "We'll come back and rig up a winch and pulley system; I've got rope in my pack back at the shore that'll do just fine. One of our pans can be a makeshift bucket, and if we can find any of yon deer, Stefan's needlework can knock us up some skin canteens."

Finding the water had lifted Danny's spirits considerably. It felt like a victory over adversity, and one of those, however small, was always welcome. He expected Ed to want to stay in this area and was waiting for a request to make this their new base of operations, so was surprised when Ed agreed immediately on heading back to the broch on the shore. Something about the wall carvings there had the lad intrigued, that's for sure, but Danny's attention was more focused on fresh meat for their supper, so was happy to see three sheep-sized deer burst out of the forest ahead of them as they retraced their steps.

Stefan, seasoned huntsman as well as shepherd, had his rifle up and aimed with practised ease. His shot downed the rearmost of the deer, but as the echo rang around them it was answered by a deep roaring bellow from within the foliage.

"That's no monkey," Stefan said.

"Something a tad bigger I imagine," Danny replied and was proved right when a beast emerged from the forest. If he wasn't mistaken, it was from the same lineage as the skull they'd seen on the wall of the broch. And he'd been right about it being a predator. In form it resembled a big cat such as Danny had encountered in Africa, but this thing was twice as big again, and following the way of things in these caverns, had three pairs of legs on which it moved as fluidly as a dancer. The tail added more to its already considerable length, a whip of muscle that looked to be a dangerous weapon in its own right, but it was the head end that had Danny's full attention. The head was almost leonine, with a shaggy mane at the neck. But the mouth reminded Danny more of wolf, being long snouted, lips drawn back showing six-inch long canines. The eyes looked to be almost wholly black, and they stared directly at the three men as the beast stepped forward to stand over the downed deer.

"The bloody thing's trying to steal our supper," Danny said. Elsa growled deep in her throat, and might have bounded forward had Stefan not held her back. Danny went to reach for his pistol, and Stefan was now raising his rifle again, but the beast was too quick for either of them. It grabbed the deer up in its jaws, turned in almost the same movement and bounded back into the foliage. The last thing they saw was its rear end, the tail whipping almost disdainfully as it took its leave.

Danny looked around in vain for the other two deer, but they had taken advantage of the situation and gone to ground somewhere further down the trail. They'd have to be lucky to see them again.

"Damn and blast it," Danny said. "Let's head back. And keep an eye out; yon beastie might fancy more than a light supper."

-ED-

Ed knew he should be keeping a lookout for the return of the cat-thing but between them Danny and Stefan had that covered and even Elsa appeared to be on full alert. Ed only had half an eye on the landscape, giving his imagination free rein as he considered the implications of finding evidence of non-human intelligence here in the deep places.

Once again he was dreaming of fame, but this time in terms of the scientific discovery, and the amazed wonder the finding would bring to the intellectual communities in the great cities. Such fame would be a long journey from their current position, trapped on an island in an underground sea with no known escape route. But the mere fact of the discovery had given Ed purpose, a desire to climb up out to the world above and show to them the secrets he'd uncovered.

"It will make Tommy's loss, if not bearable, at least more palatable," he muttered to himself, and shrugged off Danny's questioning look.

The journey back to the broch took less time than the outward walk now that they knew the way. Danny and Stefan seemed to relax more as they crossed the barren plain and Ed surmised that they were happier now that they would see an attack coming from distance rather than worrying about some big thing with teeth leaping out of the foliage. For Ed's part he was keen to hurry onward, eager to return to his inscription of the ranks of stick figures. If he could tie them in with the broch-builders, perhaps derive their meaning, it would be another notch in his belt on the way to having enough information to persuade modern science of the merits of his find. He was so intent on getting back to shore that he almost tumbled on the rocks when Danny tugged at his shoulder.

"Not so fast, lad. Something's amiss."

They stood on the small hill overlooking the promontory on which the broch sat. At first glance Ed couldn't see what had Danny so skittish; the wooden door was still in place in the doorway and the broch sat as quiet and dead as it had on their departure. Then he saw their canoe, floating offshore some two hundred yards away and getting further with every second. Again, Ed made to move forward but Danny pulled him back.

"If you think I'm letting you go into the water after it, you've got another thing coming, lad. Be still now. I'm telling you, there's something amiss."

Ed still couldn't discern what had Danny spooked but Elsa had also taken note of something; she growled deep in her throat, her gaze fixed on the doorway to the broch.

"Stay here and cover me," Danny said and strode quickly down the hill with Elsa at his heel. Stefan took out his rifle and aimed directly at the doorway. Ed unholstered his pistol and held it dangling at his thigh, trying to ignore the trembling that had suddenly risen in his fingers.

He saw Danny take his pistol in one hand and saber in the other as he approached the door. Then things happened fast. Elsa barked and launched herself full on at the door which slammed open under her attack. Ed expected something to come barreling out of the doorway in response but instead something--two things--rose up out of the open roof above the broch.

Two of the great bat-things flapped in a panicked motion, trying to gain height. Stefan didn't hesitate; he took aim and fired in one smooth motion. He hit his target; one of the bats fell back inside the broch. Danny stepped inside out of their view and they heard two more shots in quick order. Ed raised his pistol and took a shot at the second bat but it was already wheeling away. Stefan too had a pot at it, but it had risen out of range.

Elsa barked excitedly in the broch and they heard Danny's reply clear enough.

"Back off, lass. It's dead."

Stefan set off down the slope, Ed following at his heels. They arrived at the broch to find Danny holding Elsa off the body of the bat. Inside the broch their packs had been torn asunder, the contents strewn hither and thither. Nothing appeared to be badly damaged including, Ed was pleased to note, his notebook, but most of their perishable food rations were gone, obviously eaten by the bats.

Danny kicked hard at the dead beast. The body was almost man-sized, the wings each more than six feet long and almost as deep in breadth.

"What do you think, lads? Supper?"

Initially Ed was aghast at the idea.

"We can't eat that."

"Why not?" Stefan said. "To my eyes it's just a big flying rabbit. And speaking of wings…" The shepherd stepped forward to examine the beast, spreading one of the wings out and feeling at the leathery skin there. "I can do something with this… all of this. Leave it to me."

It was only then that Ed remembered the canoe. He ran out onto the shore; their vessel was now four hundred yards distant and still receding. He felt Danny's hand on his shoulder.

"It's too far, lad. You'd never reach it."

"I'm willing to try."

"I'm not willing to let you. Leave it. We must find another route."

He watched the canoe for another minute then turned away. Stefan was sitting outside the broch, large knife in hand, having dragged the bat out into the open. Ed didn't look too closely at what he was doing to the beast. Instead, he headed back into the broch. While he tidied up the contents of the packs as best he could, Danny got a fire going and soon the smell of brewing coffee filled the broch. By the time Ed and Danny had finished a smoke Stefan returned with the carcass of the bat. He quickly set up a larger version of a spit and soon the smell of cooking meat joined that of the coffee.

"I left the skin and wings drying outside. If either of you gentlemen need to relieve yourself, feel free to do so on the wings; it will cure the leather nicely. Elsa has already made a start on that."

Then there was little to do but to watch the meat cook. They talked about the events of the day, none of them able to answer Ed's questions about the origins of the broch builders. All the while Danny stood in the doorway at guard, every so often taking his gaze from the landscape to look upward.

"Remember, lads," the old soldier said. "Guard now includes up as well as out, but mayhap if we keep a fire burning, that will suffice."

Despite himself, Ed started to salivate at the prospect of the cooked meat. If it had not smelled quite so appetizing his feelings might have been different, but when Stefan announced that a haunch was done enough and cut them each a chunk, Ed wolfed it down with gusto; it did indeed taste similar to the rabbits, although there was a gamier, almost musky tang to it that reminded Ed more of goat.

While they ate, they made plans for the next day.

"With the canoe gone our options are limited," Danny said.

"We could build another," Stefan said.

"Aye, we could at that, if we find any trees big enough. We could go back along shore to the forested area, but that brings us in contact with yon baboons again, and that didn't go well for us afore. The alternative is back to where we were earlier, the forest on the slope; that more than likely brings us up against yon big cat. So we're stuck, between a rock and a hard place so to speak."

"I think we need to explore more," Ed said. "Over to the right there, where it's darker, it looks like the roof comes down close to the land again. It's probably our best chance for a way back upward."

"Aye," Danny replied. "I've been thinking the same. But the good water is over at yon volcano, so if we go, we'll go that way and take our chances with the cat... between us we've got enough firepower to hold it off."

"And by tomorrow we shall have waterskins to carry it in," Stefan said, "Then we shall not be so limited by having to stay close to it."

"We have a plan then," Danny said. "But for now we have meat, water, smokes, drink and good company. For a few hours at least I suggest we rest and make ourselves as content as we are able."

That got no disagreement from any of them; indeed Elsa, having polished off a large chunk of meat, was already asleep and farting by the fire. Ed volunteered for first watch; his mind was still too full of the marching stick figures to allow him to nod off. That too got no disagreement and soon both Danny and Stefan had joined Elsa asleep by the fire, although, thankfully, neither had yet joined in with the farting.

Ed stood at the doorway looking out, smoking a succession of cheroots. He knew from his pocket watch that it was seven o' clock and almost night somewhere high above them, but out beyond the broch it was still the same eternal twilight. More of the bats wheeled high above, over to his left and thankfully were paying no attention to the men in the broch. For the first hour of his watch, Ed worried that the smell of cooking meat might draw a predator, but all remained quiet and still, and his mind soon turned again to the stick figures.

It was a mystery that would consume him until he solved it, but any solution seemed to be a long way off. Why were there figures here but not in any of the brochs on the slopes of the volcano? And what did they signify?

Perhaps the answer lies in those black shadows to the right?

He looked forward to the morrow, and the possibility of answers.

-DANNY-

Danny woke, hand reaching for a pistol, when Stefan shook him by the shoulder.

"There's coffee and cold meat to break your fast. All is quiet."

The shepherd showed Danny the results of his handiwork during his watch; he'd stitched up three waterskins from the leathery bat's wings, each capable of holding a full gallon, with drawstrings to keep them closed and straps to allow them to be carried over their shoulder.

"You'd make someone a fine wife, my friend," Danny said, and the shepherd suddenly looked sad so that Danny immediately regretted his flippancy. Seeing his discomfort, Stefan spoke again.

"It was a fine wife that showed me how," he said. "But that is a sad story to be told when we have more liquor and fewer troubles. I promise you shall have the tale, but not today."

Stefan lay down for more sleep, Ed was deep in slumber, but Elsa was now awake, and Danny was happy of her company in the doorway as he had a coffee and a first smoke of this new day. He looked over to the right and the darker shadows; it looked to be a longish trek, more so given the need to fill the waterskins. But Danny was determined to make the effort; the old soldier in him needed action, not sitting like an old maid around a fire, no matter how comfortable.

His watch proved to be uneventful, and he had a second breakfast with the others once all three were awake.

"Only one question," Ed said. "Do we break camp from here and take our packs with us?"

"I want to," Danny admitted. "But I also realise this is the best, most defensible position we have found. I do not wish to make this decision for you."

"I trust your judgement," Ed said baldly, and Stefan nodded in agreement.

"All for one and one for all," the shepherd added. "We came to explore. Let us then be true explorers."

When they set out ten minutes later all they left behind was a cooling firepit and a small heap of bones. The remaining meat had been wrapped in some of the kelp-like weed from the shore and distributed among them. In truth, Danny's pack felt lighter than before, for he had already made inroads into his liquor and smokes supply, the meat was the only food he carried, and he'd used some, admittedly only a small amount, of his ammo. They knew the trail, the walking wasn't arduous, and there was no sign of trouble from any of the wildlife as they made their way quickly to the slopes of the volcano.

Stefan's makeshift waterskins proved to be more than adequate to the task expected of them, and all three men took turns filling up at the well. Danny winced at the extra weight when he slung his across his back to join the pack already there.

"It's going to make for harder walking, but it can't be helped," he said.

"We could leave the packs here and just take the water?" Ed said. "Establish a base in one of these brochs?"

"Perhaps later, lad," Danny replied. "We have no guarantee that we'll be back this way; best to see what lies ahead in yon shadows before we make any long-term plans. Besides, yon bats have already shown us that they're no respecters of property."

Besides, Danny's guts were roiling, his old soldier senses tingling. He was pretty sure the big cat wasn't too far away, perhaps even watching them now, waiting for an opportune moment. He needed to be moving; he'd feel less of a target that way.

THE SEA BELOW

He was proven right about the beast as they turned to walk away from the well. Danny looked back to check their rear and saw the big cat standing on the edge of the forested area some twenty paces away, its gaze fixed on him, almost eye level to eye level given its height. Danny had never looked into eyes so full of cold fury and it was only with an effort that he made himself reach, very slowly, for his pistol. He knew that if the beast chose that moment to attack, he was likely going to be dead in short order but he could at least give the others time to have their own weapons to hand.

The beast's gaze flicked from Danny's eyes to his right hand and just as the pistol came out of the holster the cat let out a snuffle and backed away to be lost in the foliage a second later.

"Bloody thing learned far too fast for my liking," Danny muttered. He turned; Stefan was raising his rifle while young Ed just stood gawping.

"If yon beastie wanted to attack us, you'd be dead now," Danny said none too calmly. "Keep your wits about you, lad; it's all you've got going for you."

Without another glance back Danny set off, his gaze set on the shadowed lands.

The trek proved longer than they could have wished, a combination of the extra weight they now carried and a trick of perspective making the shadows appear closer than actuality. They had been walking for almost three hours, and the dark lands seemed as far away as before. Danny's mood was not improved when Stefan spoke at his back.

"It follows us," was all he said, all he had to say.

Danny stopped them all for a drink of water and a smoke and scanned the ground to their rear. He saw no sign of the beast.

"Trust me, it is there," Stefan said. "A shepherd can read the signs. Elsa knows it too; she has been walking at heel and staying close these past twenty minutes. Her flock is in danger."

Although he looked long and hard, Danny was unable to see any sign of the cat, but he trusted the shepherd's judgement. When they finished their smokes and started to walk again five minutes later all three of them had their weapons at hand, ready to react in an instant to any trouble.

They walked in silence for a while as the trail they were on grew ever more barren, the rock underfoot so dry that even the tough wiry grasses could not take root in it. The temperature rose again, a damp heat that had all three sweating and Elsa's tongue lolling. And still the land in the dark shadows ahead seemed little closer.

"Perhaps this was not the best idea," Ed said, his voice coming in gasps.

"We are not going back," Danny replied. "Not with yon beast on our heels."

Ed waved off to their right and the distant shoreline.

"If we cut across from here, we could be at the shore broch in an hour."

"And then what? Yon beast will still be following us, the bats might have returned, hell, we might even have the pleasure of the company of a horde of curious baboons. At least here we can see what's coming at us."

"And if it gets warmer?"

"Then we sweat. Come on, lad. Pick up the pace. We'll need a longer rest soon and we have to find a spot that's not quite as exposed."

After a further hour's sweaty walking, Danny noticed that the light had dimmed, it now being akin to a late evening if they were up above and beneath the stars. When he looked up, he saw for the first time that there were definite structures in the gloom ahead, tall spires of jet black stone, far larger than any broch, that reached like stalagmites towards the roof, some indeed almost seeming to touch the rock above at their highest points. The towers, more than a score of them, did not look quite man made, yet neither did they look to be entirely natural, being a strange amalgam of both and obviously smoothed and corroded by time. As they got closer, they saw what appeared to be windows set at intervals up the columns, and doorways in their bases leading to vast spiralling staircases in the interiors.

"And who built these then?" Danny asked. "It certainly wasn't bloody baboons."

"Possibly the same people who built the brochs," Ed replied. "Although the stonework here looks more sophisticated… and much older. These must predate the pyramids of Egypt by centuries...millennia even."

"I don't care how old they are," Danny replied, looking up to where the columns tickled the roof. He pointed at the third column on their right. "That one goes all the way up...and so will we. It might be our way topside, and I for one am eager for some sun on my face. But first things first...rest and a smoke are in order, I think. Come on."

Danny led the others to his chosen column. It was some twenty yards wide at the base, tapering as it rose up into what was almost total darkness at the roof of the cavern. A wide doorway at ground level led to a short hallway and a narrow, steep, stairwell leading upward. Ed made to drop his pack in the hallway.

"No, lad, not here," Danny said. "The doorway is too exposed, too wide for three of us to cover.

Let's head up the stairs a bit… see if we can find a spot that can be defended."

It proved to be cooler inside the tower, a welcome respite from the dead, still air of the cavern floor, and got cooler still as they ascended the first flight of stairs. They didn't have to go far to find a spot that Danny's trained eye found acceptable as a defensible position. After thirty steps they came to an opening. The stairs continued upwards, hugging the exterior wall, but the opening led into a circular chamber with a single, tall narrow window on the opposite wall from the entrance. The chamber itself was empty, just bare stone walls with no sign it had ever been inhabited.

"This will do nicely,' Danny said. "There's no kindling, so there'll be no coffee, but we have meat, water and somewhere safe to have a kip. We'll rest here before going up higher; yon steps are going to be a sore trek; they were built for someone with longer legs than mine."

Danny saw that Ed wasn't listening; the younger man walked the circumference of the room, studying the walls.

"They're here too," he said, almost to himself.

"What's that, lad?"

Ed motioned at the wall.

"The stick figures, like in the broch. They're faint, worn with age, but they're here too."

"Aye, very nice I'm sure," Danny said. "But I can't see them being of any use to us. I'll leave the esoteric to you, lad. As for me, I'm concerned with more practical matters. It's been a long walk on a hot day. I'm keen to get on up but the auld legs need a rest first. What say we get some grub and kip here before moving on?"

"Elsa agrees," Stefan said, laughing and pointing at where the dog had already laid herself out to sleep below the window.

Danny stepped over to look out at the view. There were more columns close by and beyond them a dark shore with an even darker sea beyond; they were almost at the furthermost tip of the island and travel any further in that direction was going to be impossible without a light source. That brought a chastened silence to them all when he called the others over to have a look, the scene serving to amplify their solitude here in this strange land.

"Chin up, chaps," Danny said. "We know this tower reaches the roof. There's going to be a way up for us. I feel it in my bones."

In actuality all that Danny felt in his bones at the moment was a deep ache that he was more than happy to appease by sitting down with his back to a wall.

They each ate from their portions of the bat meat; they'd get one more meal each out of it, then they'd need to find more food, but Danny hoped to be somewhere much higher, much nearer the 'real' world before it came to that.

After eating, Stefan lay down beside Elsa beneath the window and was soon asleep. Ed had taken to studying his little figures on the wall. To Danny's eye they looked like primitive scratchings, no more, no less, and he failed to see the younger man's fascination in them.

"At least it keeps him out of mischief."

Danny took first watch, standing in the doorway smoking. There was nothing to see but the stairs but he had plenty of things to occupy his mind, hope being among them.

-ED-

Stefan woke Ed six hours later and Danny woke up at the same time so that all three broke their fast together; the very last of their hard biscuits and water followed by a smoke. There had been no signs of anything occupying the tower apart from the three men and the dog; the 'night' had passed quietly. If the big cat was still on their trail, it was too cautious to approach such a well defended position.

The water was too warm, the biscuits too dry but Ed barely noticed. He missed his coffee but the sleep had rested his weary legs and now he, like the others, was eager to get onto the staircase and head upwards. If they could find an easy route back to the surface so much the better, for on future trips Ed, and the world's scientific community beside him, would be able to come and go into this new realm at their leisure. It was a nice dream to entertain as they prepared to move out.

When Danny led them out to the stairwell, Ed was right at his back, with Stefan and Elsa bringing

up the rear. They quickly realised that Danny had been right; the steps had been made for beings with a larger stride than was comfortable for any of them, although Elsa seemed to be enjoying the almost bounding gait she had to employ to ascend. After only a dozen or so steps, Ed's calf muscles were already beginning to complain and he was grateful when they reached another landing and another room off it, giving him a momentary respite.

This new chamber was much like the last; although the window was differently positioned the room was just as empty, and yet again there were faint imprints of marching stick-figures on the walls. Danny didn't give them any time for examination. He was already stepping up into the next portion of the stairwell. As Ed joined at his back, he noticed it was now getting noticeably warmer again, accompanied by a new odor, an oily tang in the air, thick and cloying in nose and throat.

"I smell it, lad," Danny said when Ed spoke up. "But if a bit of a stink is all we have to cope with, I'll take it and be thankful."

They kept climbing, their breath coming heavier, the air getting warmer and the strange smell growing to a noxious stench; it seemed that the air wavered in rainbow colors around them.

When Danny stopped at another landing and went to light a smoke, Ed stayed his hand.

"Gases in enclosed spaces are not to be trusted," was all he had to say. Danny nodded and put the match back in its box, turning his attention instead to the chamber that opened up off the landing. This was much like the last, but this time the window overlooked the length of the island they had walked to get here, and more besides. Ed stepped up beside Danny for a look.

They had already climbed high enough to get a panoramic view. Their first home here on the island, the broch on the shore, was clearly visible, as were the structures on the slopes of the volcano. Past that the forest stretched away the length of the island until, way off in the distance, a dozen miles and more distant, the land became rocky again. There was something there, wavering in the vaporous air, something that might even be more dwellings, but it was impossible to tell in the haze. On either side of the island the underground sea stretched away, dotted on the right-hand side by more islands that all looked to be rocky upthrusts with no vegetation to be seen.

"Let us hope these bloody stairs lead somewhere," Danny said at Ed's side, "because it looks like we're here or nowhere for the duration."

Any hope they had was dashed several flights of stairs later. The noxious odor became so strong that all three of them walked with their hands covering noses and mouths and Elsa gave out deep growls in her chest. Danny stopped abruptly on a landing and that led to Ed almost walking into him. Ed saw why they'd stopped when he looked over the old soldier's shoulder; the upward path ahead was blocked, the stairs coated knee-deep with what looked to be a semi-solid black tar from which rose an oily vapor that glistened in an aurora of rainbow colors. Ed guessed this to be the cause of the smell that was afflicting them.

Elsa went forward, sniffed at the tarry mass, then backed away fast, whimpering.

"Don't touch it," Stefan said. "She knows trouble when she smells it."

Danny looked at the stairs, then into the chamber off the landing. There was a window there, looking out onto the dark area at the bottom end of the island.

"Give me a hand here, lad," Danny said, and hoisted himself up onto the window ledge. The walls were almost a yard thick, and Ed held Danny's legs while he leaned out to look upwards.

Danny took several seconds, then dropped back down into the chamber.

"Bugger," was all he said, and motioned that Ed should look for himself.

Ed scrambled up into the window and leaned out carefully, avoiding looking down lest vertigo get the better of him. The upward view didn't do much for him either. The roof of the cavern was twenty yards or so above them. The structure they had climbed did indeed reach the top, but only because the roof had come down to meet it. The rock above was coated thick with the black tar and it had oozed and dripped down over the turret, like melted candle wax, covering the whole structure above them.

"There might be an exit up there among this black shite," Danny said, "but I'll be buggered if I can see a way to get to it."

Ed didn't answer. Suddenly he was thinking of melted wax, of gases in enclosed spaces, and lit matches. He had an idea.

"What if it's flammable?" he said. "Could we burn our way up?"

"Are you daft, lad? We'd get roasted."

"Not if we're careful," Ed said. "We stand well back, lob a lit rag at it, and leg it way down the stairs...at least one of us does; the others will be well down the stairs already in case of an explosion."

"Explosion? Listen to yourself, lad. This is madness."

"I'm open to other ideas," Ed said. "As you said, it's here or nowhere, and I'm none too keen on playing Robinson Crusoe. We're close to finding a way up. Will we ever get any closer? Isn't it worth the risk?"

He saw that both the other men were skeptical.

"Look, I'll do it myself," he said. "I'm faster on my feet than either of you in any case. You two back away, as far as you want, just don't get in my way if I'm on my way down after you with my arse on fire."

Danny finally saw that Ed was not to be swayed from the idea.

"We'll take your pack and water," the old soldier said. "Best you be as unencumbered as possible. Give us five minutes then do your thing. Just don't get yourself fried."

A minute later Ed was standing alone on the landing. Several minutes after that he was as ready as he was ever going to be. He'd wrapped a handkerchief around one of their spoons and set it alight from a lit match. He had a bad moment as the match flared, hoping against hope that it didn't immediately spark a conflagration, then managed to breathe as the cloth took light.

He counted to three, backed off into the downward stairwell, then lobbed the lit material at the mass of tar. He didn't wait to see if it took; he'd already turned and was bounding down the stairs.

A blast of heat almost knocked him off balance then he was leaping precariously down the twisting stairwell with the fires of hell lapping at his heels.

-DANNY-

By the time Danny, Stefan and Elsa emerged at the foot of the structure the top was already well alight. Fire showed at the windows several levels below the roof and flames rose up to roil across the rock above. Black smoke, forming like a thundercloud on a hot day, spread out to cover ever more of the ceiling, darkening the already dim cavern and sending scores of the giant bats swooping away in search of clearer air.

"Oh, lad, what have you done?" Danny whispered.

They waited in the doorway at the foot of the stack, watching for Ed, the heat increasing with every passing second until it came down the stairwell like a blast from an opened furnace door. Ed came with it, flames licking at his heels.

"Run, you idiots," he shouted, and almost knocked Danny over as he barrelled past him.

Then all three were running, Elsa leading them on, full-pelt, away from the tower as smoking black tar flowed out like a river and flame washed the whole height from ground to ceiling.

They ran for almost a quarter of a mile before having to come to a halt to catch their breath. Danny turned and looked back at what was now a conflagration. Black smoke hung across all of the cavern roof at this end of the island, laced through with guttering red flame. Burning streams of the black tar oozed and dipped from high and all of the turrets were now ablaze at the top, a grotesque parody of a birthday cake. Below that, flames lapped at all the windows and more of the tar oozed out of the doorways of the stacks, already spreading out across the plain towards where the men stood.

"Any more great ideas, lad?" Danny said.

The drips of flaming tar from on high were getting more persistent. They were also getting much closer.

"It's not going to burn out any time soon," Ed said. "I think a strategic withdrawal is required."

"But where to?" Stefan answered. He was looking up to where flames were spreading out in a blanket across a wide expanse of the roof above them. "Is anywhere safe?"

Danny didn't waste any time coming to a decision.

"The broch on the shore is closest. If worse comes to worst we can retreat to the water, the shallows at least, and hope that nothing else tries to kill us."

The light had dimmed even more, the cavern taking on a reddish, flickering hue. Smoke was now mingled with falling flakes of ash as the flames reached the vegetated area of the ceiling and fed greedily. The heat was stifling and Danny felt the skin of his cheeks stiffen as if taken by sunburn.

"Move," he shouted. "Double time, unless you want to be baked to a crisp."

The next half hour was a journey through hell; if Danny had been a religious man he might well have taken it literally. The fires above, rather than abating, were growing in intensity. Burning ash and drips of flaming tar came from above while flowing, oozing black tar swallowed the ground at their rear. The whole bottom end of the island behind them was a single wall of sputtering flame. Giant bats swooped and shrieked in a terrified frenzy and the only saving grace was that the beasts were too busy trying to survive to pay any notice to the three men and a dog who fled shoreward beneath them.

Stefan stumbled, fell, and let out a yelp of pain when his palms flattened on steaming hot rock. When he got to his feet his hands were red, blisters already rising.

"Faster," Danny shouted, setting his gaze on the shore that was still a mile distant.

They ran.

Around them their world burned.

Danny was surprised to reach the shore; it was touch and go. It felt like the clothes on his back were on fire and he was pretty sure his feet were blistered inside his boots. Elsa was running with a noticeable limp, pained whimpers every few steps. Ed looked to be almost on his last legs, his face red with exertion, his breath coming in great noisy whoops and Stefan stumbled along in a bent-over crouch that almost had him on all fours.

Danny was in the lead as they crested the hill above the shore and had to force himself to come to a halt. They had been beaten to the peninsula; he looked down across the narrow causeway to see the huge cat beast prowling around the perimeter of the broch, snarling and growling at the burning ash that fell around it. Danny looked to Stefan, expecting to see the shepherd raise his rifle, but the weapon turned in the man's burned hands; he was unable to lift it to take aim.

The delay in Danny reaching for his pistol almost proved fatal. The beast had seen him and launched itself into a full-on attack, as if blaming the men for its fiery predicament. Danny was aware that Stefan had pulled Elsa aside to prevent her trying to come to their aid and Ed had thrown himself aside to the ground, even now rolling and reaching for his own pistol. As for Danny, the old soldier in him would not allow him to do anything other than stand his ground.

Everything slowed down for Danny. The act of drawing his gun seemed to take forever as the beast, maw open and teeth showing, leapt in a seemingly impossible jump up from the causeway, coming directly at him.

It was the old soldier's instincts that saved him. He brought up his pistol and turned in one smooth action, showing his back to the beast and firing under his left armpit in the same movement. He didn't know if he'd hit his target for it immediately felt like a wall had fallen on him. He felt sudden wetness at his neck and shoulders.

Blood. The damned thing's had my neck open.

Then, as quickly as it had come, the weight lifted. He heard a roar of pain, then someone had him by the shoulders, turning him over. Danny looked up to see Stefan waving the tattered remnants of a waterskin in his face.

"My handiwork saved your life, my friend," the shepherd said with a smile. "Although I fear it is now beyond even my repair."

Danny rolled to his feet and looked back over the plain to see the big cat bounding away through the smoky gloom and falling ash.

"Did I hit it?"

"The bloody thing was moving so fast I couldn't tell," Ed said at his side. "But at least it has buggered off."

"For now," Danny said, then winced as a burning hot flake of ash tumbled down like a snowflake to land on his cheek. He looked up to see a sky full of falling embers, some of them still burning.

"Quick. To the water. At least it'll be cooler there."

The whole ceiling above them was a roiling mass of black smoke and flickering flame. As they ran down the slope to the water's edge hot ash fell around them. The whole island to the left of them was nothing but fire. Danny strode into the water, its coldness providing immediate relief. He stopped wading when the water reached his thighs, not wishing to get his pack or ammo belt wet. He saw that the others were equally circumspect except for Elsa who was paddling around them in apparent delight.

"Stay close to shore, lads," he said. "This might feel safer, but we all know it's not."

Without waiting for a reply, Danny began to wade, staying five yards from shore, heading away from the still encroaching fire. With water only up to his knees he was able to holster his pistol and use his freed hands to make up a cigarette. The absurdity of breathing in more smoke during such a conflagration wasn't lost on him but the old habit did much to calm his frayed nerves, rooting him back in some semblance of reality while the cavern went to hell over and above him. Stefan had also slung his rifle and was carrying Elsa in his arms, with young Ed bringing up the rear. The fall of ash was getting steadily heavier, and hotter, burning their scalps and charring their clothing on shoulders. Danny had to throw water over Stefan's pack to extinguish a small fire that bloomed there.

"We need to get out of this," Ed shouted.

"I'm working on it, lad," Danny called back. He surveyed the shoreline. On their journey up the island to this point in the canoe he had spotted numerous cracks and small crevasses in the cliffs; he just had to find one that would provide them with enough shelter.

They had been paddling for ten minutes before he found one he liked; an outcrop of the cliff overhung the sea over a flat bed of rock above the waterline. They wouldn't be able to stand, but they could sit comfortably, possibly even lay out to sleep, and the rock above would protect them from falling ash. It was as good as they could hope for in the circumstances.

Danny led them under the rock. Stefan put Elsa down and she paddled eagerly over and pulled herself up onto the flat rock. She barked, as if in enthusiastic agreement at Danny's choice. He took that as a good sign and climbed out to join her before giving the others a hand up onto the rocky shelf.

"Make yourselves comfy, lads," he said, looking back out across the sea to where the ash fell steadily, some of it hissing as it hit the water. "We could be here for a while."

They managed a basic meal of the last of the bat meat and water. Danny longed for coffee but at least he had his smokes and what was left of his liquor; that was enough to bring him some small degree of contentment while they sat staring out at the scene out on the water.

Everything beyond their small cave was now tinged in a red hue and although the air was cooler here it was still almost stiflingly hot.

"I wasn't to know," Ed whispered at one point. "How could I know?"

"Don't take it on yourself, lad," Danny replied. "We all agreed to your wee plan. Who were we to know it would be so flammable?"

"It's a tar bubble of some kind, it has to be," Ed replied. "Who knows how long it has existed, trapped there in the old stone?"

"Aye. And the Lord only knows how big it might be or how long it will keep burning. What's done is done, lad. If we were to spend time questioning every bad decision we've made...including the one to come here in the first place...we'd be here from here to eternity. Get some rest. If it doesn't stop soon, we're going to have to venture out again, ash or no ash, for we will need to eat."

After that there was little to say. Stefan and Elsa stretched out and were soon asleep. Ed sat by Danny's side, both of them smoking, neither speaking while the black ash continued to fall and the sea glowed red in reflected flames.

-ED-

At some point Ed slept, his dreams full of stick figures marching through fire while a distant drum beat mercilessly. He woke with a start when Danny shook him by the shoulder.

"We might be out of the worst of it," the old soldier said.

Ed sat up and looked out over the water. The fall of ash had lessened considerably and the red glow was nowhere near as prominent on the surface. It was still almost too hot to breathe but a cooler breeze coming from off the water promised an end to that.

"It seems we are to live, for a tad longer at least," Danny said. His accompanying laugh woke Elsa into a bark that also woke Stefan.

"What say you, lads? Are you ready to see what damage we have wrought in this land?" Danny said.

Ed wondered whether he'd ever be ready but gathered his pack and gear and followed Danny out into the water when the old soldier moved out. Ed emerged from under the rock to find Danny standing, opened mouthed, looking back along the island towards the broch on the shore.

The roof above was mostly dark, black even; what little light there was coming from areas behind and to their left where the flames thankfully hadn't reached. But everything to their right and in front of them had burned; there was only blackened rock to be seen over the whole right half of the island. In the distance, what had been stacks reaching all the way to the roof were now only tar covered blackened stumps. The only fire yet visible came from above these stumps where tar still dripped, flaming all the way from ceiling to ground. Apart from that everything was a fire-blackened wasteland; what little vegetation had clung to the ground here had been replaced by tarry black ash.

Ed looked to Danny for guidance.

The old soldier pointed away along the shore to their left.

"You saw it from the window; there's a possibility of more dwellings up that far end. And they may well have been spared the fire, given that there's still light over that way. We should go there."

"We'd have to stick to the water."

"Aye. It's that or go through the foliage where the baboons live. Neither fills me with any excitement. But what choice do we have?"

What choice indeed?

Ed realised that his thrill of exploration had gone, burned away in the fires, leaving behind the simplest of desires in the need for food, water and safety. Any other thoughts would have to wait.

"If I get a say, I suggest we try the forest," Stefan said. He was carrying Elsa again. "I cannot bear her forever, no matter how much I would want to, she cannot swim forever, and to allow her to walk means shallower water than this."

Ed looked along the shore to their left. In the near distance he saw that the blackened ground gave way to an area where the pale foliage still dominated.

"We are armed, and forewarned," he said. "That is more than enough to see off a pack of angry monkeys. I agree with Stefan. Let us seek a path ashore. As you said, we need food, and there's little to be found standing here."

"I like a man who thinks with his belly," Danny said, and laughed again.

The old soldier's continual good humor did much to sustain all of them as they headed to their left and waded closer to the patch of forested ground.

They stayed in the water for another five minutes until they came to a spot where the cliffs receded to a rocky beach that made it easy to go ashore. Elsa yelped in excitement when Stefan put her down and bounded away among the rocks like a frisky puppy. The men took the opportunity to pause for a smoke and a swig of water.

They were at the edge of the extent of the fire's reach; above them the ceiling was slightly blackened, but with patches of the luminescent vegetation hanging overhead. The bats were returning, soaring in wide circles near the roof and down on the land there were patches of charred foliage amid the ashes. The heat was less than it had been before and Ed was glad of the easier walking when they made their way up the shore.

Elsa returned as they reached the edge of the forest, pleased with herself and carrying a charred lump that turned out to be what was left of a rabbit. It was badly burnt on the outside, but the meat itself was perfectly cooked. Ed wolfed his portion down; he hadn't realised how hungry he had become.

"Hopefully there's more where that came from," he said.

"If there is, she will find it," Stefan said as the dog, having taken her own portion in one bite, bounded away into the foliage again.

Ed eyed the forest warily. Everything appeared quiet but he remembered all too well the frightening ferocity shown by the baboons on their last encounter. He noted that Danny had his pistol in hand again and Ed unholstered his own weapon as they left the shore and headed into the foliage.

Thankfully it proved to be relatively easy walking. Although leafy, the vegetation wasn't stiff and could be pushed aside with ease. They followed what Ed took to be a deer trail judging by the amount of droppings underfoot. It led them farther from the shore, deeper into the woods. A quiet calm fell around them, disturbed only by the occasional rustle from where Elsa bounded off to their left. The foliage was partially burned in places, but the deeper they went in the less evidence of the flames was apparent and soon even the smell of smoke and ash was only a memory. On looking up Ed saw that the ceiling above was a carpet of the lank bioluminescent roots; they were out from under the area that had been aflame.

Danny appeared to be in little mood to allow any relaxation. The soldier led from the front, using his saber to hack and slash any foliage that dared to get in his way. Ten minutes in, Elsa returned with another rabbit; this one wasn't burnt, and newly dead. Stefan stashed it away in his pack, and over the next half hour the dog returned with two more. After that she didn't roam but kept close order at Stefan's heel. Danny continued to set a brisk pace, only coming to a halt after an hour's walk when they climbed up only a rocky outcrop that for the first time gave a clear view of the journey ahead.

They had a view over this end of the island. Below them the foliage stretched away for several more miles, then gave way to rockier ground on which there was a settlement of some kind, a large collection of scores more of the broch-like structures, some still intact, others long since tumbled and broken in ruin. Beyond that, at the farthest extent of the land, a larger building stood on a promontory out onto the sea, a tiered castle of black rock that looked to be almost pyramidical. The township was still something in the vicinity of five miles away but the mere sight of it had Ed's curiosity rising again, but Danny held him back from plunging ahead.

"I don't know about you, lad, but I've worked up a hunger. Let's have some of yon rabbit and a rest."

Ed stood, gaze fixed on the township ahead while Stefan and Danny got a fire going and a spit turning. Soon the smell of the cooking rabbit drew his attention back to the fire. He went to join the others.

While waiting for the rabbit to cook, Ed wondered aloud what might be waiting to be found at the settlement ahead.

"I wouldn't pin much hope of finding much of anything," Danny said. "There's nowt here but wild animals. The builders are long gone, surely you know that?"

"There may be artefacts," Ed said.

"Aye. And there may even be boats... or had you not considered that?"

In truth Ed hadn't given any thought as to the possibility, but now that it had been mentioned he could think of little else. A society capable of the buildings they'd seen would surely have also taken to the water? Excitement grew in him at the possibility and he hardly tasted the rabbit once Stefan cut their shares and handed it out. By the time they'd all finished, then had a drink and a smoke, Ed was more than ready to head at full speed for the castle on the promontory.

"Not too hasty, lad," Danny said. "Just because we haven't seen them it doesn't mean those bloody baboons aren't around. And yon big cat too... we need to keep our heads and not go dashing about.

We've got a load of this forest to traverse yet. Hold your horses."

Danny was proved right about the need for caution almost as soon as they descended from the outcrop and re-entered the forest of leafy foliage. Elsa's hackles rose and she gave out a deep growl in her throat. Somewhere in the forest ahead of them something screeched. It was answered by more screeches farther to their right.

"We do not like these monkeys," Stefan said.

"No, we don't," Danny said. "Give them a volley."

Ed's pistol bucked hard in his hand as he fired in the direction of the second set of screeching; Stefan's rifle boomed like a small cannon blasting a patch of foliage to scattered shreds and Danny fired smooth and practised, three quick shots towards the first screeching. The gunshots echoed around them. Ed's ears rang for long seconds, then once again the forest had fallen deathly quiet. High overhead one of the great bats squawked in confusion at the gunplay, but down at ground level nothing moved.

"Well, we've given them something to think about. Let us hope it is enough. Double time and stay in close order, lads. The sooner we're out of this and into clear ground again the happier I'll be."

Danny didn't wait for a reply but plunged ahead along the deer trail. Ed followed right behind him, with Stefan and Elsa bringing up the rear. For the first five minutes Ed thought their shooting might have frightened off the baboons entirely but Elsa began growling in her throat again and, although there was no more screeching, Ed couldn't shake off the feeling that they were being followed, tracked by things just far enough deep in the foliage to remain hidden.

"Aye, lad," Danny said. "The wee bastards are still there, just a bit more cautious of us now. Eyes peeled and pistols ready...if they attack en-masse it could get messy quickly."

-DANNY-

Danny didn't want to worry the younger man unduly, but their situation was more perilous than he'd let on. The pack of baboons must be at least a score in number given the shadows he kept seeing flitting through the foliage on either side of them. They moved silent and fast, a practised hunting troop. Danny had seen a unit such as this in Africa. That time it had been chimpanzees but these beasts here moved with similar guile and intent. That time he'd seen them taking down an antelope the size of a horse. He didn't think these things here would have much trouble with three men and a dog.

Our only hope is that they're more scared of the guns than they are hungry.

The further they walked into the jungle, the smaller that hope became, especially once the deer trail narrowed so that the foliage was brushing up against Danny's shoulders as he pushed through it. Once again, he had to resort to using his saber as a machete. Having to hack through the foliage meant he made much more noise than he was happy with; the baboons didn't have to do much work to keep track of their position. Indeed, the new sounds emboldened the hunting party. Shadows crept closer around them and more than once Danny heard excited yelps, although those were quickly stifled. Danny knew the paces and beats of a successful hunt. Normally he was the one doing the stalking but here and now he knew that they'd reached the point where an attack could come at any second.

He couldn't take the tension much longer and when the trail opened up slightly ahead of them into a small circular clearing some five yards across, Danny came to a decision and strode to the central point of the cleared area.

"Bugger all of this creeping around for a lark," he said. "To me, lads, back to back. We make a stand here. Let's show them who's boss in these parts."

Stefan moved to Danny's left, Ed to the right and Elsa took guard between Stefan's legs. Danny had his pistol in his right hand, the saber in his left. Every nerve in his body felt alive but his aim was steady as he took aim into the foliage.

"Come on then, let's have you," he shouted.

The attack came without warning. For two heartbeats it was quiet, the next the foliage itself seemed to burst into life as the baboons launched themselves out of it. There was no time for thought.

Stefan fired first, almost at Danny's left ear, then the clearing was filled with the roar of gunfire and the wild screeching of baboons.

Danny's first shot almost took the head off one, his second blew a hole in another's chest, then they were on him. He shoved his pistol halfway down the throat of another before firing and hacked two limbs off another. He had to duck as Stefan, swinging his rifle like a club, swatted two more away, caving their ribs in the process. Elsa was below him; she had one of the baboons by the throat, worrying at it as if it was no more than a barn rat.

And still they came; Danny's estimate of a score had been too low and although some of them had paused to tear and feast on their own dead, still more came leaping out of the shadows. Danny clubbed another on the head with the butt of his pistol, feeling its skull collapse as it fell away only to allow space for another that was on him before he could get the saber around for a cut at it. Two pairs of limbs wrapped around his waist amid a howling fury of thrashing upper limbs. A screaming maw of a mouth shrieked in his face. It was within an inch of ripping off his nose when Danny managed to get the pistol around into its ribs. He fired, kept firing until he clicked on empty, and then had to tug the dead thing off him and toss it aside.

His blood was well and truly up now, all thought of caution thrown to the wind as the stench of blood and the roar of battle brought the soldier to the fore. He strode into the mass of baboons like an avenging angel, howling a battle cry of his own as the saber swung and cut and butchered. All pretence at defence abandoned, Stefan joined Danny, bellowing like an angry bull, still swinging the rifle like a club, scattering the baboons left and right while Elsa harried at them.

Finally, the baboons retreated in the face of the men's fury, or at least tried to. Danny and Stefan pressed forward and kept at them all the way across the clearing to the edge of the forest, both of them yelling like men possessed. Danny only stopped hacking when it was obvious he was only cutting through the fleshy leaves.

The baboons were gone, leaving twenty or more of their number as dead and butchered corpses behind them.

Danny and Stefan yelled in triumph, before realising that Ed was not joining them. The younger man was in the center of the clearing on his knees, with a dead baboon in front of him and blood dripping off his nose from a bleeding scalp wound.

"Dashed thing tried to rip my hair off while I was still wearing it," Ed said, his face pale but his eyes full of the fire of battle. Danny clapped him on the shoulder.

"You'll live, lad. Come on, up you get. Get your pistol reloaded; we've got to move out before those buggers come back."

Two minutes later Danny led them out again. The trail was wider here and he strode with more purpose than before. It had been a victory. Only a small one, but hope had been rekindled.

They reached the edge of the forest with no further incident. From here flat, rocky ground stretched away towards the settlement and castle at the far end of the island, with no sign of life save the hardy grasses scattered here and there in cracks in the rock. Danny didn't slow.

"The boy needs stitches in his wound," Stefan said. "The bleeding will not stop."

"Let's get to one of yon brochs first," Danny said. "I'd like to have walls around me in case the wee bastards get our scent again."

By the time they reached the dwellings, Ed was white as a sheet and unsteady on his legs.

"The castle," the younger man said, "I can make it to the castle."

"Nope," Danny said. "That delight can wait. You need that wound looked at, then food and rest, in that order."

The first broch they came to was too much tumbled in ruin, but the second was as solid as their previous shelter on the shore, a bonus being that it had retained a sturdy door despite its centuries of being uninhabited. Danny raided a third broch, breaking its old door down for firewood and soon they had a blaze going, a spit turning with a rabbit on it, and Stefan had his sewing kit out, showing off his needlework skills on Ed's scalp.

Danny stood in the doorway, pistol in hand, staring out across the open ground to the forest, then raising his gaze to the fire-ravaged area beyond. Flames flared in the distance, tarry drips falling aflame from a still-burning roof but for now the worst of the fire had burned itself out. It had left behind an even darker cavern at that end of the island and a burnt taste in the air that even a cigarette couldn't dispel completely.

"We need a plan," Danny said without turning. "Ever since we got here we've been lurching from one crisis to another. That stops now; I'm in charge of my own destiny, dammit. I do not live at the whim of a roaring fire or a colony of bloody baboons."

Stefan replied first.

"As for myself," he said, "I miss my flock and the feel of sun on my face. If the plan is to find the quickest way back up top, then it will get my vote."

Ed surprised Danny by agreeing with the shepherd.

"The sooner we get back, the happier I'll be," he said. "We have been ill-prepared for voyages such as this. I will know better next time."

"Next time, don't tell me about it," Danny replied. "I intend to be too busy with women and liquor to help out. But yes, the plan is to return to our lives. I am open to suggestions as to how to proceed from where we have managed to get ourselves."

Ed came and joined Danny in the doorway. Stefan had shaved away several inches of scalp above his left eye and thick black stitches held together the lips of a two-inch tear in his flesh. But the lad at least had some color back, although his eyes were sunk in deep shadows and he looked like he hadn't slept for a week.

"You mentioned boats," Ed said. "I think that's our first priority."

"Are you willing to trust our luck to the water again? With yon big serpent boogers around?"

"It's either that and attempt a return back to the shore we left, or live out our lives on this rock, isn't it? Unless there's another option I haven't considered?"

"No, you have the right of it. There's risk in any direction. At least if we die on the water, we die trying to get home. As I said, I prefer to be in charge of my own destiny, so boats it is then; we'll search yon castle and environs first as that'll be our best chance. But even before that, you need to rest, lad. You're out on your feet."

It was a sign of just how tired the lad was that Ed didn't argue, just went back to sit with Stefan by the fire.

They had to wake Ed up to give him a share of the rabbit once it was cooked and he was asleep again soon afterwards as a result of a hefty swig of Stefan's brandy.

The shepherd shook the skin bag sadly.

"Almost gone," he said.

"Aye. My whisky is likewise depleted. I've got plenty of tobacco left, so there's that at least."

Danny was back in the doorway on guard. Stefan came to join him, Elsa deciding to lie down by the fire with Ed. The shepherd passed over the near-empty skin of liquor.

"You mentioned women, my friend," Stefan said. "Is there one in particular, perhaps waiting for you even now?"

Danny shook his head.

"None. I have been too busy playing the soldier to settle down. First I was too young, then too far away from civilised ladies and now, probably, too old. But I have seen things most men can only dream of. I would not swap the life."

Stefan waved a hand to encompass the view over the island.

"And you are still seeing them, even now. As for myself, there was a wife, once. I said before it was a story for later. Well, it appears it is later. Shall we finish this brandy? I might not get a chance to tell it again."

The shepherd had finally articulated what Danny had been refusing to do; there might not be too much of life ahead of them. Danny made up two smokes and passed one to the shepherd who lit it and took a deep draw on the brandy before speaking.

"She was my… how do you say...sweetheart. I knew her as a lass in our small school, and she had my heart even then. Seventeen we were when we were married. We were never blessed with children, but that didn't matter. We had each other.

For nearly twenty years we had each other. It wasn't long enough."

Stefan stared into the fire and Danny thought he was done, but then he spoke again, even quieter.

"She died at my feet. It was as if a thunderbolt took her; one second she was in the kitchen talking to me, the next she was on the floor, her eyes glazed like a china doll, her chest silent. I tried all the tricks I have learned from rescuing the flock on the hills, but none would bring her back. The doctor said her heart had given out, but I think God took her because she was too good for this world."

He fell silent again, tears rolling down his cheeks, but he still wasn't done.

"I said I missed my flock. That is true. It has been all that sustains me since she left. But there is something here too that stirs the blood. Although I am still only miles from where I have been most of my life, this feels like an adventure. I think she would not begrudge me it."

Danny touched his bloodied tunic, where he still wore the blood and tissue of the baboons, there having been no time to wash it off.

"A dashed bloody adventure at that," Danny said. "But I know what you mean, and so does the lad there. Even if we do return to hearth and home, this place will keep calling him back. And despite what I said earlier, I would return with him, if he asked it of me. And I'd be dashed glad to have you at my side."

Danny raised the skin of brandy and shook it.

"There is just enough for a last toast together. To adventure!"

He took a swig and passed it over. Stefan was about to reply when their conversation was interrupted by a sound from out in the jungle.

The roar of the great cat echoed across the island.

-ED-

Ed woke with a pounding headache like a drum bearing inside his skull and inadvertently bought himself a flash of white pain when he touched his fingers to the sticky scalp wound.

Danny was asleep on the other side of the fire, while Stefan and Elsa guarded the door.

Ed groaned as he pushed himself to his feet, having to stand still for several seconds before he was sure he wasn't going to fall back to the ground.

"I can take watch for a time if you need some sleep?" he said, but the shepherd shook his head.

"I had a spell earlier; you have been out for many hours, my young friend. And if truth be told, you look like you need more time yet to recover."

Ed moved to pass Stefan and head outside. The shepherd blocked his way.

"Danny said no," Stefan said. "The big cat-thing is on the prowl. It is all I can do to stop Elsa throwing herself into the fray; I do not need to be looking out for you too."

"I merely want a look at that castle," Ed said.

"To quote our sleeping friend, the castle can wait. Ease yourself, rest. There is more of the rabbit, there is water and we have tobacco although the brandy is sadly gone. Be content, for a time at least. I have a feeling we will need all of our strength in the days to come if we are to escape this place."

Once Ed saw that the shepherd would not be swayed, he contented himself with a survey of the interior of this broch. It was built on the same principles as the others they'd seen, and here too there were row upon row of the stick figures. He retrieved his notebook from his pack and compared the figures on these walls with the ones he'd transcribed earlier. It didn't take long to notice that there were definite repeating patterns common to both sets but he still had no clue as to what these might represent, or why they were inscribed on the walls of the dwellings.

He was still mulling over the problem when Danny woke and stretched.

"A good morning to all," he said, laughing. "What does a man have to do to get a beer around here?"

"If it is in fact a good morning," Ed replied, "then on our return I shall gladly stand for beer all day back in that bar in London where I found you."

"Now then, that gives me something to strive for, lad," Danny said, rising. "And it gives me impetus to get started. Are you hale enough to take a wander over to yon castle?"

"I am ready when you are."

Danny sniffed at his armpits and touched the dried gore on the front of his tunic.

"Now all I need is a bath."

"I think we could all do with one," Ed answered, laughing, realising that he too was liberally coated in blood, although in his case it was mostly his own.

They broke camp ten minutes later. They met no resistance while making their way through the settlement and reached a causeway that stretched off for fifty yards, sea on both sides of a two-yard wide stone track that had been built of the same stone as the brochs. They took the opportunity to bathe, two staying on watch while the other washed, fully clothed, trusting on the warm air to dry them off once back on land. While Ed was washing off the blood and grime, he took the opportunity to look across the causeway to the castle that waited for them.

It too was built of the same basaltic stone as the brochs but this had clearly been a much larger, even monumental, operation. As he'd noted from afar, in outline it looked almost pyramidical, but now they were close he saw it was rather a series of circular tiers atop each other, each of diminishing size, rising like an expensive piece of wedding confectionery to a central spire on top of which was a balconied chamber looking out over the expanse of sea.

Not for the first time Ed wondered what manner of hands, if there had even been hands as he knew them, had built this place, and in what long aeons past. By the time the others, Elsa included, had finished their ablutions, Ed was champing at the bit to see what might lie inside.

In contrast to the towers at the dark end of the island the way up the castle walls was via an exterior stairwell, there being no obvious entranceway into the main structure; they circumnavigated the whole structure just to make sure. Neither did they find any boats, nor any evidence there had ever been a harbor or quayside.

"Looks like we go up," Danny said. "If nothing else, it looks like a spot we can defend."

Ed studied the steps warily. They were set on the same pattern as those in the dark turret, having been built for something with a longer stride length than a man. But they were wide enough to traverse safely, almost enough for two of the men to ascend side by side. Before taking the first step, Ed studied the stonework of the walls and was almost disappointed to see none of the serried ranks of stick figures, no carvings of any kind, only cold black stone.

They fell into what had become their standard positions, with Danny taking the lead, Ed in the middle and Stefan bringing up the rear with Elsa at his heel. There were five levels, each one of them in itself a walled fortification; the only way an attack could take the building would be by using the stairs. At one time there had been heavy wooden gates at the top of each flight but they had long since fallen prey to time and hung, rotted timbers on what was left of thick ropes.

"They'll make good firewood if nothing else," Danny remarked as they passed the gate for the second level. Before continuing up the steps Danny went farther along the walled walkway to take in the view. They looked down across the whole length of the island. Ed tried to trace the trail they had taken on their journey here; he looked past the forest, to the slopes of the old volcano and past that to the land newly blackened by the fire that he had set. Apart from a pair of the great bats spiralling lazily far above there was no sign of life save themselves. Ed wondered if the baboons ever roamed into this settlement, then pushed the thought away; he'd seen more than enough of the monkeys without wishing them any closer.

He saw that Danny was looking away to the open sea on their right. There was a commotion several hundred yards out. The great bats swooped and dived like seagulls, plucking what Ed took to be fish from the water's surface. And amid the turmoil on the water, pale backs of serpent things rose and fell, showing great tail flukes as they dived, gaping maws as they surfaced to swallow fish by the bucketful. He counted six separate serpents, each distinguishable by the shape of their backs or notches on their flukes. These waters were more populated than they had imagined.

"I've seen this before," Danny said. "Off the Cape. Feeding frenzy the boat's Captain called it. Of course it was whales and gannets then but it looks like the behaviour is the same."

"Whatever it is," Stefan said, "it shows us the water is not safe to venture upon."

"Aye. We knew that already though," Danny said, and without another word headed for the stairs to the next level.

By the time they reached the top, Ed's calves were complaining and his headache had returned with a vengeance, a pounding like a great drum in his skull. Danny led them up and into the high chamber with the balcony. The only thing above them now was a tapering spire. They were high enough to see the farthest extent of the underground ocean far off in the distance, the same cliffs from which they'd set sail what seemed like a lifetime ago now. But Ed's eyes weren't on the view, they were on the center of the balconied area. At first he took it for a firepit, but as he stepped closer he saw it was an internal passageway, a tight spiral staircase going down into the depths of the castle. It was pitch black down there; they had passed no windows on the way up, and from the echoes, Ed guessed that this stairwell went all the way down in total darkness.

The pit itself was rimmed in stone, a foot-high circular wall some four yards in diameter. Most of the stones were the same black rock they'd seen everywhere, and these were carved with the rows of stick figures Ed was by now expecting to see. Only one stone was different, it being almost white, a polished, squared off piece of what looked to Ed like quartz. There were no carvings on the stone, but its top had been smoothed, as if having been rubbed down over time by use.

Danny leaned over the dark pit. He slipped a bullet from his belt and let it drop. They heard it clatter and clang, ringing like a bell on the way down. It kept going for a long time before the sound faded.

"There's no way in hell you're getting me down there," Danny said to Ed. "Just in case you were thinking about it."

"Why would they build it like this? It's a strange kind of castle altogether," Stefan said.

"I don't think it's a castle at all," Ed said. "If I were to guess, I'd say it is some kind of temple; a place of ritual in any case."

"What manner of pagan thing might they have been worshipping in here?" Danny said.

"I don't know," Ed said. "But the answer is in these bally stick figures, I know it is."

"That's all very well," Danny said, "but it gets us no closer to home. Let us rest here for a spell. Then we have decisions to make, but first, food and a smoke I think."

They took Danny's suggestion, used the old wood and ropes as kindling, and got a fire going there on the top level where they cooked the last of the rabbit, finished off one of their two waterskins and Danny shared the last of his whisky. Rations were getting perilously low and they all knew it, yet none spoke of it as they stood at the balcony wall, looking out over the sea and smoking while the rabbit cooked on a spit in the chamber.

-DANNY-

"As I see it, our priorities remain the same," Danny began after they'd seen off the rabbit. They were sitting around their fire, smoking. "There may be no boats, and building one might not even be possible given what we've seen of the vegetation here. But I can see no other recourse but to try."

"It is a chain of islands," Ed said. "There may be more tall turrets reaching to the roof farther down the archipelago. We need not traverse open water, at least not for too far."

"Aye, lad, but we'd be doing it in the dark under yon burning area. Might be better just taking our chances with the serpents for at least we'd have a chance of seeing them coming."

Stefan pointed to the well in the room's center.

"What about down there? It may lead to deeper caverns?"

"And it might just be what it appears to be; a black hole going nowhere. Too many mights for my liking. But first things first. We need more food, more water. I'm going out for a while; you should stay here."

"What happened to not splitting up?" Ed said.

"That was then. This place is defendable and away from any signs of trouble. Don't worry about me."

Danny turned to Stefan.

"I'd like to take Elsa though, if she'll come. She'll scare out a rabbit if there's one to be scared."

Stefan agreed, although Danny saw that Ed was still skeptical.

"There's no other option, lad," he said. "Besides, I've got the saber and my pistol. We've given yon monkeys plenty to think about, and I don't intend going anywhere near the forest. I'm going to spend an hour looking for rabbits and, if possible, water. I'll be back before you know it."

He didn't wait for an answer; Danny was afraid the lad would talk him out of it, and even more afraid that he'd succeed.

Elsa followed unbidden at his heel as Danny went out to the stairs. When he looped round to see the view down the far end of the island, he saw that their problems were about to get worse than just a lack of food and water; the fire had flared up again, insistent streams of tarry flame falling from the roof in a fiery waterfall. And this time the flames were taking hold in the forest on the slopes of the old volcano; it was only a matter of time before the whole island would be aflame. To make things worse, if that were possible, dark smoke was once again creeping across the roof of the cavern, sending the great bats swooping and shrieking in a frenzy. It was growing dimmer by the second.

Danny gauged the risk of the spread of fire against their need for food and decided he should have maybe an hour's grace, enough time for Elsa to do her thing, enough time to find some water that didn't have the metallic taste of that in the ocean around them.

Although neither will do us much good if we are to be roasted to death.

By the time he reached the foot of the castle he realised that his estimate of an hour had been wildly optimistic. Flames snaked across the roof and had now reached previously unburned patches of vegetation above, causing a recurrence of falling ash that was already beginning to coat the ground like black snow.

"Elsa, fetch me a rabbit," he said.

The dog knew what was expected. She bounded away across the causeway to the rocky area beyond and her excited yips and barks told Danny she was on the hunt. Danny decided that a search for water wasn't going to be productive; the fall of ash was getting stronger by the minute and a wash of heat came on a breeze from the far end of the island. He looked across the open ground to find Elsa to call her back and saw that another problem had been added to the growing list; the forest of foliage was also now well alight across the whole width of the island. Driven out by the fire, the huge cat-beast loped across the open ground. Behind it, Danny saw spooked deer scattering and, beyond them, a troop of baboons several score strong chasing them down.

It was the big cat that had him most worried though; it was heading Danny's way, coming at some speed.

"Elsa, heel," he shouted. "To me, girl."

He lost the big cat in a dip in the ground, then heard it, a roar that sounded like triumph.

"Elsa!"

He was about to head to the dog's defence when Elsa came up out of the same dip in the ground. She had a rabbit in her mouth and the big cat on her tail. By the time Danny drew his pistol and saber they had almost reached the far end of the causeway.

"Come on, girl," he shouted. Elsa needed no encouragement; she was running full pelt, and the cat was mere yards behind her. Danny couldn't risk a shot. He was as likely as not to hit the dog. He retreated toward the stairs, hoping to get a clearer shot from higher up, but knew even as he moved that he wouldn't be given the time. Elsa was already halfway along the causeway and the big cat was closing in on her. He saw the cat tense, getting ready to pounce and knew it was now or never.

Trusting his nerve and his eye, he raised the pistol, aimed and fired in one swift movement then had to leap backwards for the stairs as Elsa almost barrelled into him. Danny tripped, fell on his backside and just had time to get his saber up in front of him as the big cat leapt. The impact as it hit him drove Danny back against the stone, sending a flare of pain in his back that had him wondering whether it was broken. He felt the saber go in all the way to the hilt, felt heat as the beast's blood poured over his hand. The beast's body engulfed him totally in warm blackness. He heard Elsa barking somewhere in the distance but the blackness was getting deeper, the sounds fainter. He tried to bring his pistol to bear but his hand was trapped.

The blackness called to him as the full weight of the beast fell over him.

He went to it.

-ED-

Stefan was first to react when a shot rang out from somewhere below them and was just ahead of Ed when they reached the top of the stairs. Ed had a blocked view of the foot of the stairwell, only enough to see Elsa worrying at the neck of what looked to be a dead big cat, but he heard the dismay in Stefan's wail.

"Danny!"

Then they were both bounding down the stairs, uncaring of the fact that a single slip might send them tumbling in a mess of broken bones. The shepherd reached the bottom just ahead of Ed and it was only then they saw a bloodied, outstretched leg poking out from under the body of the beast.

"Help me!" Stefan shouted, and began heaving at the carcass. It took both of them to roll the dead weight aside and more time to get Elsa to back off, which she finally did, but only to stand six feet off, growling deep in her throat.

Danny lay on the bottom step. His eyes were open but glazed and there was no sign of movement.

"Is he dead?" Ed whispered.

"I hope not, my friend."

When Stefan bent to check, Ed finally noticed that the cavern had darkened considerably and when a falling ember made him blink, he thought to look up.

The whole roof above them was a carpet of black smoke interlaced with snaking flame. Black ash fell like snow.

"Stefan?" Ed said, almost afraid to ask.

"He lives," the shepherd said. "But I cannot tell if his back is broken. If we move him, we might kill him anyway."

Ed pointed up at the flames.

"If we do not, we may all be dead soon anyway. At least up top we have some degree of shelter."

Stefan looked up, then down at Danny.

"I hope I am doing right by you, my friend," he said. He bent and, with a strength that belied his stature, hefted the old soldier over his shoulder.

"Fetch the weapons," Stefan said. "He may yet still have need of them."

Both pistol and saber lay in a large pool of rapidly congealing blood and were sticky to the touch. Ed wiped them off on his shirtsleeve and followed the shepherd back up the stairs. Elsa came at their back, carrying a dead rabbit proudly in her jaws.

By the time they arrived at the topmost chamber, Stefan was breathing heavily and the black ash was falling in a curtain to carpet the stairs. The air inside the chamber tasted warm and burnt but once inside they were, as Ed had hoped, protected from most of the falling embers.

Stefan lay Danny down on the floor and at that the old soldier groaned and his eyelids flickered. He still didn't wake but Ed took it as a sign that it was more of a possibility than he'd thought minutes earlier. Ed lay Danny's pistol and saber on the floor beside the prone man, not knowing what else to do with them. When Stefan poured some water from the skin, Danny's lips opened to take it, another good sign, but he hadn't moved a muscle below his neck since being lifted and Ed was starting to have serious worries about a debilitating back injury.

Stefan turned to Ed.

"Watch the stairs, lad. The big cat is dead but there might be other things out there seeking such shelter as this place provides."

Ed drew his pistol and went to the doorway. There could be a horde of baboons climbing the stairs right now and he'd never be able to tell; the black fall of ash obscured everything more than a yard outside the door. The air was noticeably warmer here too, hot and dry in his throat, so much so that he could only take it for a minute before having to retreat back inside. Once there he noticed that there was a cool breeze coming up from the well in the chamber's center.

"We should go down," he said, turning to address Stefan. "We can at least avoid being roasted."

"That is a good idea, lad," the shepherd replied. "But moving Danny more than we have already is risking too much. Let us wait to see how he fares when he wakes."

"If he wakes," Ed thought, but didn't say. Neither of them were ready to hear that.

Ed stood as close to the doorway as he dared, trying to peer out into the gloom. Darkness was gathering fast, a blackness laced with intermittent flares of red. It looked like the whole cavern beyond the boundaries of their small chamber was aflame.

Ed heard a ripping tear and turned to see Stefan making a makeshift firebrand from pieces of his shirt and one of the timber shards from the old doorway they used as kindling.

The attack came as soon as his head was turned.

A baboon launched itself through the ash fall and leapt directly for Ed's face, teeth bared and talons reaching. Ed was so taken aback he had no time to react, but luckily Elsa's reflexes proved faster. She too leapt and knocked the monkey out of the air mere inches from Ed's face. She had it pinned to the ground and its throat ripped out while Ed was still reaching for his pistol.

Lucky for him that he did so, for a second baboon came out of the ashfall, at ground level this time on all fours but coming on fast, heading, not for Ed but for where Elsa worried at the corpse of the first. Ed's first shot took the beast in the throat, sending warm blood flying. That was the cue to bring on frenzied screaming from out in the darkness on the stairs.

Ed sent three more quick shots out the open doorway. Stefan came to stand beside him, a firebrand in one hand, Danny's pistol in the other.

"Steady, young friend," the shepherd said. "We cannot allow them to get in here; they would overrun us."

Another baboon leapt at waist height from the darkness; Ed saw that its fur was scorched and burned from falling embers of ash. That was all he had time to notice before Stefan put a bullet in its brain and it fell in the doorway at their feet.

"They're burning alive out there."

"Better out there than in here," Danny said from behind them. He turned to see the old soldier push himself to his feet by leaning on his saber. Danny looked at the flame-flecked darkness beyond the door, then down into the black depths of the well.

"Do you still think there's something down there, lad?"

"Do we have any choice?" Ed replied, pointing at the doorway and the inferno beyond.

The baboons' barking and yelping from outside spoke more now of pain than of anger, and finally their flight and fear of the flames overcame their reluctance to face the men's gunfire. Four of them came through the door at once, a blackened, smouldering vision of hell's teeth and fangs. Ed took one, Stefan another, the third tripped on its fallen comrades and had Elsa at its throat before it could rise, and Danny, obviously hampered by the injury to his back, still had enough of his old soldier's instincts to step forward and skewer the fourth with his saber.

The heat from the doorway was getting more intense by the second. The skin at Ed's cheeks tightened.

"If we're going, best do it now while we have a chance," he said.

Danny responded by kicking their discarded packs down the well. He took his pistol from Stefan and pointed down into the dark.

"Stefan and Elsa lead the way, then you, lad. I'll be right behind you, so no slacking."

Ed followed the bobbing light of the shepherd's firebrand down into the dark.

-DANNY-

The cold air in the well provided welcome respite from the stifling heat above but it proved to be perilous going underfoot, the steps once again having been built for a longer gait than Danny possessed. Every footstep brought a new jarring pain in his bruised back and his neck strained with the effort of continually looking back up the stairwell to ensure no fresh attacks from the baboons.

As the size of the aperture above seemed to dwindle, so too did it take on an ever-more red hue, and waves of heat from above vied with colder air coming up from below. Slowly but surely the heat was winning; Danny was raising a sweat.

He took another look back and saw a humanoid, six-limbed figure outlined against a fiery background up above. He fired two shots and the baboon fell away, but it had still been alive which concerned Danny mightily.

"Faster, lads," he called out. "We're not out of this yet."

He had to up his own speed to keep up as Stefan's firebrand bobbed downwards ahead, then almost ran into Ed when the shepherd stopped. He saw the man bend and lift one of their packs from where it lay on the steps, then they were descending again as the heat from above washed over them.

Danny had no time to give any thought to looking up for they were almost running now, bounding down into blackness with no thought of tripping in an attempt to outrun the inferno they'd left behind.

"We must be near the bottom," Ed said. "Unless I've lost count of the steps."

"What makes you think there is a bottom, lad?" Danny said, panting in the heat. "We haven't found the other packs yet; they're still somewhere below us."

That fact was solidified in their minds minutes later when Ed called out again.

"That's it. We've definitely come down farther than we went up on the outside."

They were also, finally, starting to descend faster than the heat from above and Danny felt a most welcome cold breeze on his face once again.

"This air is coming from somewhere," he said. "Let us hope it is hospitable."

The descent became a personal hell for Danny. Despite the fact that they appeared to have escaped the roasting hell above, every step downward was a battle with pain. Danny had once marched most of a day with a fractured leg; this descent was giving that a run for its money as the worst walk of his life. It felt like crushed glass was being pushed into every muscle from his instep to his shoulders and it was all he could do to refrain from crying out as waves of pain washed through him, threatening to send him back into a deeper darkness than that in which they descended. He was almost happy when Stefan called out from below.

"I think this is as far as we go."

Seconds later Danny joined the others in what appeared to be the bottom of the stairwell.

It opened out into a wide chamber, cathedral-like given the echoes coming from around them. Stefan's firebrand only allowed them a circle of light a few yards in diameter. All else was pitch-black, with no sign of windows.

"Yon breeze is still coming from somewhere," Danny said. "Let's follow our noses."

By studying the effect of the breeze on the firebrand they were able to pick a direction. They found the rest of their packs almost immediately, but Danny was unable to get his onto his back.

"Rest, friend," Stefan said, hefting two packs. "I will manage for a while."

Danny followed, feeling every day of his age, while Ed took charge of the brand and led them across a smooth expanse of stone floor that was clearly built, not naturally formed.

They found the source of the colder breeze within minutes.

It originated from an area of stone wall three yards wide and several yards high, drilled with hand-sized holes at six-inch intervals across its width some eight feet off the ground. The breeze was coming through these holes, but if it was indeed a door there did not appear to be any mechanism with which to open it.

"End of the line," Danny said, and slid to the ground to sit with his back to the door. He got out the makings of a cigarette and started to roll, wondering whether this might be the last time he ever performed the almost automatic task.

Ed, to his credit, wasn't ready to give up. He began to inspect the walls on either side of the door, holding the brand close to the rock face.

"There are more of those figures here," he said. "Many more. It means something, I'm sure it does."

"It means we're done for, lad," Danny said. "Here, sit down and have a smoke with me."

Ed wasn't listening. He moved farther away, leaving the others in darkness.

"Hey, there's something here," the younger man called out seconds later. "You need to see this."

"I really don't, you know," Danny replied, then groaned when Stefan helped him to his feet and more pain lanced up and down his back. He half-walked, half-staggered over to where Ed had bent over something sitting between the floor and the wall.

At first Danny took it for the skeleton of a man, albeit a singularly large one. Then he saw the extra arms, two of which were holding onto what Danny took to be a circular box, similar to a lady's hatbox. Something about it had Ed excited, and it took several seconds for them to get the lad's meaning.

"Don't you see?" Ed said, but in truth Danny didn't see much of anything at all, and that only served to animate Ed even more.

"It's a drum. It's a bally drum, and the stick figures aren't a code; they're the markings of a rhythm."

"Very nice," Danny said. "But it doesn't get us out of this hole."

"Maybe it does," Ed said, then went quiet.

Stefan joined Danny in sitting, back against the impenetrable doorway having a smoke. Elsa lay between them, looking as if she did not have a care in the world. Ed, meanwhile, had prised the drum from the dead man's bony hands and was sitting a few feet to their left, the guttering brand propped up at his side. He had his notebook open on top of the drum and was tapping out a series of beats on the instrument's side that echoed around them like rapid footsteps in the dark.

Danny did not see how this would avail them of anything, and was about to say so when Stefan put a hand on his shoulder.

"Let the boy be," he said. "We all deal with this in our own way. This is his."

"Aye, I suppose so," Danny said, and showed Stefan his cigarette, "and this is mine, although I'd give my left bollock for a drink right about now."

"I would give your left bollock for one too," Stefan said, deadpan.

-ED-

The other men's laughter echoed long and loud around the chamber but Ed scarcely noticed, lost in a search for the rhythm that would unlock the secret of the marching stick figures. He knew it was there, somewhere in the ranks of sketches in his notebook; what he had to do was find a starting point. He figured that a figure with no limbs or head meant a pause, that one with all present meant seven beats, and he thought he could figure out all points in between that easily enough. But getting the beat right continued to elude him.

Then, as he was on the verge of giving up, his fingers and his sight and the figures on the page all seemed to align. He drummed out eight bars...and the chamber responded by echoing them back to him exactly one beat off the tempo. The more he drummed the louder the echo became, the sound taking on resonance and depth as if there were not one but a whole orchestra of drummers beating out the rhythm. The chamber rang, echo building upon echo until Ed felt a vibration reach him even through the stone floor on which he sat.

He looked up to see Stefan and Danny rise from their position, both of them looking around uncertain as to what was happening.

As for Ed he was lost in the rhythm, his palms slapping the drum, the notebook having fallen unheeded to one side. It was now as if he was following the beat rather than leading it, his drum only one among the many, the room itself taking up the primary role in the ever-rising pounding. He felt it permeate him, through his palms, up his arms, into his chest where his heart seemed to beat in time, lost there in the dance.

It was Elsa's barking that brought him somewhere closer to his senses, although even then he did not lose a beat in the drumming. When he looked over he saw that the great stone doorway against which the others had been sitting was sliding to one side in a series of jerks in time with the pounding rhythm that filled the cavern. The cold breeze quickly became a wind, so fierce that it blew out Ed's brand like a puff of breath extinguishing a match. Ed was surprised to note he could still see the others; thin light came through from beyond the still opening doorway.

Danny's shout reached him above the cacophony of the drumming.

"Get your arse over here, lad, before it shuts on us again."

Ed laid down the drum in order to get to his feet; that seemed to signal the end of something, and the beginning of something else. The great stone doorway began to jerk closed in time with the still echoing beat of now distant drumming. Stefan, Danny and Elsa had already moved to go through to the other side.

The door was closing fast.

Ed broke into a run, made it just in time and had to throw himself through a gap that was only just wide enough to fit through.

The stone slammed closed at his back and the distant echo of the drumbeat finally fell silent.

"That was too close for comfort," Ed said, then realized that neither of the others was paying attention to him. He saw why when he turned from the door and saw where they stood.

A cavern, greater in size even than the one they'd left above them, stretched away as far as they could see, lit from a high roof festooned with the now familiar bioluminescent vegetation. A flock of great bats circled high above. The men stood on a shelf atop a sheer cliff some five hundred feet high.

That wasn't the most remarkable thing.

The cavern floor, stretching away for many miles in every direction, consisted of a great city of black stone, with well marked streets and avenues, terraces and archways, buildings as great as any of the ancient cities of antiquity, temples and marketplaces, fortified walls and terraced gardens.

There was no sign of life anywhere.

THE STORY WILL BE CONTINUED IN
THE CITY BELOW

Check out other great
Dinosaur Thrillers!

P.K. Hawkins
THE LOST ISLAND

Scientists Dr. Eccleston and Dr. Lerner have done many routine expeditions for the Skurzon Corporation in the past, helping the company search the ocean for newly available resources freed by melting ice. They're expecting to maybe find oil at the bottom of the Arctic Sea. What they aren't expecting is a lost island that defies all scientific understanding. When something comes out of the sea and destroys their research vessel, the scientists and the rest of the crew are forced into a game of survival against forces no human being has ever seen alive. If they can survive the giant insect swarms, the man-eating plants, and the dinosaurs, they might be able to live to tell the tale. But when each passing moment reveals murderers in their midst, their survival starts to look less and less likely.

William Meikle
THE LAND BELOW

A treasure hunt into the deepest cave system in Europe takes a turn for the worst.Now rather than treasure it is survival that is at the forefront of the spelunkers' thoughts. But their attempt to escape out of the dark deep places is thwarted. Men are not at home in the depths. But there are things that are, pale terrifying things. Huge things.Things red in tooth and claw.

SEVEREDPRESS

@severedpress
/severedpress

Check out other great

Dinosaur Thrillers!

Greig Beck

PRIMORDIA: IN SEARCH OF THE LOST WORLD

Ben Cartwright, former soldier, home to mourn the loss of his father stumbles upon cryptic letters from the past between the author, Arthur Conan Doyle and his great, great grandfather who vanished while exploring the Amazon jungle in 1908. Amazingly, these letters lead Ben to believe that his ancestor's expedition was the basis for Doyle's fantastical tale of a lost world inhabited by long extinct creatures. As Ben digs some more he finds clues to the whereabouts of a lost notebook that might contain a map to a place that is home to creatures that would rewrite everything known about history, biology and evolution. But other parties now know about the notebook, and will do anything to obtain it. For Ben and his friends, it becomes a race against time and against ruthless rivals. In the remotest corners of Venezuela, along winding river trails known only to lost tribes, and through near impenetrable jungle, Ben and his novice team find a forbidden place more terrifying and dangerous than anything they could ever have imagined.

William Meikle

THE LOST VALLEY

A remote high valley in the Canadian Rockies hides an ecosystem that has been lost in time. A small team of prospectors and their local guides are looking for gold. What they find is blood and terror and death.The valley's monstrous inhabitants are not about to let go of its secrets lightly.

 SEVERED**PRESS**

 @severedpress
/severedpress

Check out other great
Dinosaur Thrillers!

Doug Goodman

HUNTING WITH DINOSAURS

A hunting party is sent to catch and kill raptors that have escaped Dinosaur Falls Restricted Area and murdered nearby hikers. But the hunters find the raptors are unlike any creature they've ever hunted, and soon one lone bowhunter is running for his life through the Perdidos Mountains. He discovers an old wilderness survival trench and burrows in deep, but eventually the raptors come for him. His only salvation is to befriend a wolf hellbent on destroying the raptors. If they can come together, they can form a pack the world has never seen, but if they fail, the raptors are waiting with their sharp teeth and elongated claws...

Edward J. McFadden III

DINOSAUR RED

There's a doorway on Mars that has mankind's greatest minds perplexed. Deep beneath Aeolis Mons an ancient secret is revealed, and a team of explorers led by Forest Judge, Deputy Commander of Gale Base Alpha, are dispatched to investigate. The prehistoric gateway reveals a biosphere preserving Earth's distant past, and as Judge and crew stand on the threshold of mankind's greatest discovery the Martian ground trembles. A roar thunders from within, the doorway closes, and the team is trapped. Six mission specialists, each with unique skills, each with different reasons for wanting to break free of the primordial trap. To get home Judge is forced to choose between escape and changing the course of humanity. What will he do?

Made in the USA
Coppell, TX
19 June 2021

57706052R10083